AT DADDY'S HANDS

Courage Knows No Age

JACOB PAUL PATCHEN

Black Rose Writing | Texas

ISBN: 978-1-68433-344-8
PUBLISHED BY BLACK ROSE WRITING
www.blackrosewriting.com

Printed in the United States of America
Suggested Retail Price (SRP) $16.95

At Daddy's Hands is printed in Garamond Premier Pro

DEDICATED

To those who are currently enduring the torments of sexual/physical/mental abuse, to those who have braved the harassment of this evil, and to those survivors who have outlasted that hell. This is for you.

THANK YOU

To my family for the love, support, patience, and guidance when I needed it most. Thank you to those courageous people who submitted their true stories to the back of this book. I hope that your voices roar. A very special thank you to Nikki Foster Russ for all of her time, energy, patience, and support on this project. Nikki, without you, this book would not be what it is today. Thank you to Jason Hillyer for the artwork. Thank you to my readers, my friends, and my hometown of Cambridge, Ohio for the continued support, love, and daily inspiration that you graciously give to me. Finally, I thank the Lord for blessing me with the ability to bring awareness, help, and change through my words. It is a privilege and honor to write for you.

MESSAGE FROM THE AUTHOR

For a couple of years, I worked as an Activity Director/Case Manager in a mental and behavioral health facility for adjudicated youths, ages 13-17. During this time, I worked alongside therapists, case managers, and parents to correct dangerous thinking, build life and social skills, and break patterns of mental, physical, and sexual abuse.

Working both with inpatient and outpatient clients, I was able to see firsthand the effects that sexual assault has on children and their families. As tragic as it is for many of these children, it's what they know as normal behavior. For many of these children, they had endured years of sexual, mental, and physical abuse, believing that it was *their* fault. They considered it punishment for behaviors that they had done rather than understanding it as their abusers' wrongdoings, that it was their abusers' mental illnesses or evil intentions that caused them harm. It took months and years of counseling to build their self-respect, self-confidence, and trust back up.

Many of these children had abused their own siblings, family, or friends of the family in the same manner in which they were abused by their fathers, mothers, uncles, or family friends. You see, the biggest revelation that occurred to me while working in this field was that sexual/mental/physical abuse is a long chain that stretches down through the family. In most cases, it is a learned behavior that had happened to the abuser at some point in their life, and most likely, from someone that they knew. Their father did it to them because his father did it to him and his uncle did it to him, and now he does it to his sister or brother or cousin. Sexual abuse is a terrible and sickening cycle.

I have witnessed a system that has failed these children. I have monitored family visits between the abuser (father) and the victim (twelve-year-old female) that were allowed by the court because the evidence was not substantiated. I have witnessed self-harm and suicide attempts, escapes and run-aways. I have seen a system that would rather penalize its employees than try to help the victims of these crimes.

There is such a taboo associated with sexual assault that people are afraid to talk about it. People are afraid to discuss what to do if someone becomes a victim of sexual assault. Adults shake off the signs, because "that couldn't happen in *this* family, *this* school, or *this* community." But, I assure you, it happens everywhere. And there are abusers out there that are getting away with it because we enable them, through lack of intervention, inaction, and lack of prosecution. In some cases, criminals are more likely to do more time in jail because of drug-related crimes than sexual assault or abuse.

How do we allow this to happen? How can our system be so inhumane? Folks, it's up to us to change that.

My aim here is to build up the courage and the strength to be able to break that mold, to snap that chain. I want any victim or survivor that is reading this to know that **you can get through this.** I realize that the system is damaged, that the policies are strict, and that the odds are against you. But I have seen success. I have witnessed children break through that mold and change the outcome of their family's history. I believe in you – because I know that there is strength within you. I know that your abuser has sucked the life right out of you, left you confused, terrified, broken and ashamed. But hear this, there are those of us who are on your team; there is so much support out there, whether it be teachers, coaches, counselors, family, friends, or groups and programs... there is an army in your corner. But it is up to you to break that link. It is up to you to ring that alarm.

And I believe that you are strong enough, brave enough, smart enough, and beautiful enough to fight it, and win.

Please note: This is a fictional story placed in a real town. In no way am I trying to draw negative attention to the small town that I grew up in. I love this town, this small area, and all the close-knit people in it. In no way am I trying to bring negative attention to the police, judges, or anyone else in this town. I have many friends that are in law enforcement, and I know them to be exceptional people. But, by naming a real place, I felt it would make the story more impactful. But, either way, fiction or not, this is a very real and **everyday issue** that we need to come together to solve.

AT DADDY'S HANDS

Courage Knows No Age

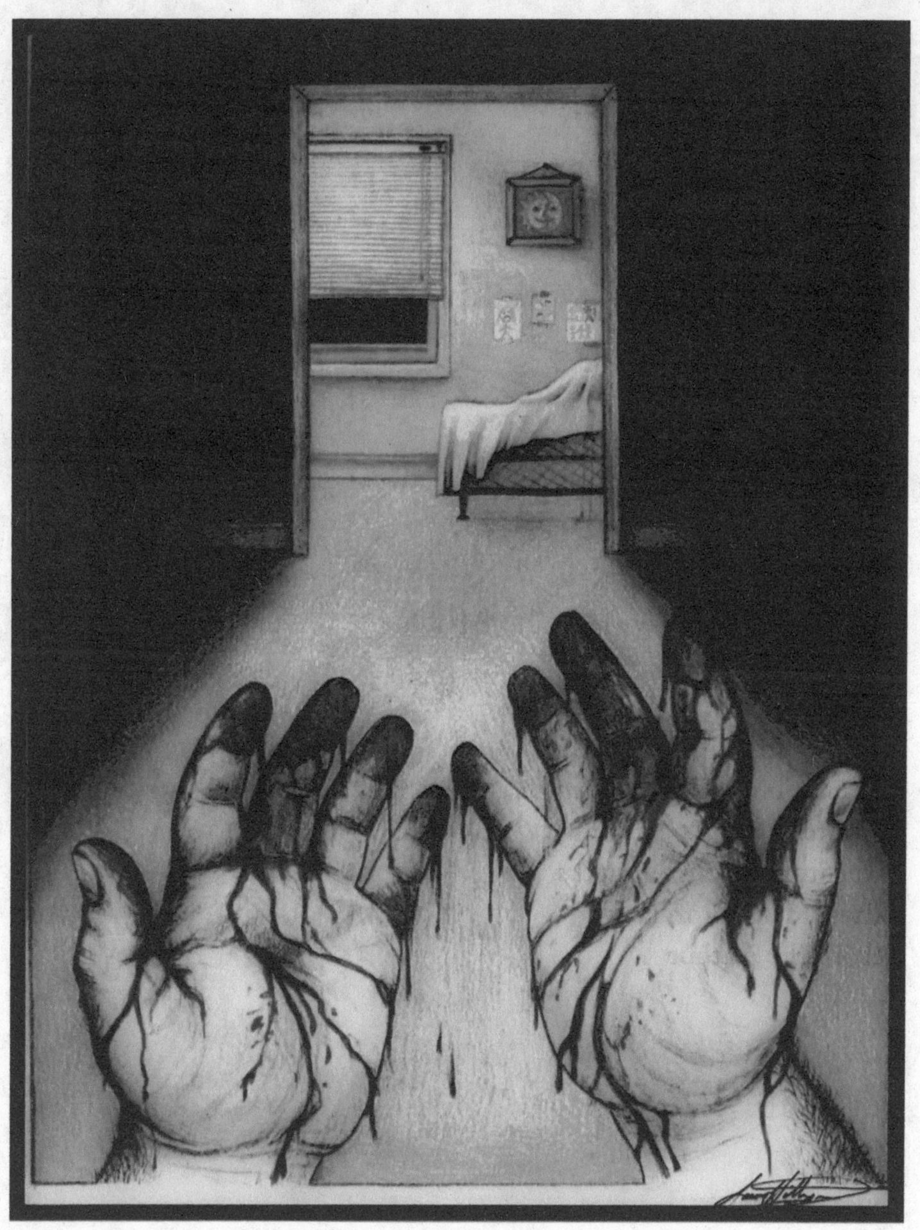

CONTENTS

ONE.
THE ASSAULT

2018, October

Jim Handler had just shoved his way through a mess of shoes, book bags, and jackets piled in front of the door. It had been another long and trying day at work. Home didn't make things any better. Depending on which way he leaned, the house smelled of either burnt toast, fresh dirt, muddy sweat, or spilled wine. His right hand was clenched when he slammed the door shut.

"Damn it, Ashley! What the hell do you do all day?"

A sinful darkness replaced the evening glare and stretched down the hallway. Jim basked in it for a moment. It was only the flashing light from the TV in the living room to his left that snapped enough light through the small walkway for him to see Tyler's muddy football pants wadded up with his practice jersey and nearly on top of Jim's good pair of Nike sneakers. The round, matte black clock in the hallway, still missing the battery cover from the last time it was knocked from its nail, crept its way past 5:37 p.m.

Ashley turned up the volume to a rerun of *The Bachelor.* She was still in the same thing she wore to bed: a pair of black sweatpants and an oversized, grey, Meadowbrook Football sweatshirt that read in orange letters *One moment, One day, One game: One Chance.* Her tangled blonde hair was in a loose, messy bun, thrown together with a deep sigh after a quick glance in the bathroom mirror at the dull bruising on her left cheek from her husband's tempered right hand last week. The kids were already dressed, fed, and at school, by the time she finally lifted her fuzzy, fleece blanket from her pounding head and hazel, bloodshot eyes. Annoyed, she groaned at the bright morning light as she crawled out of their king-sized bed at 10:43 a.m. on this glaring October, Thursday morning.

She looked at ease; her small, frail frame curled up on the new leather sofa, black to match the half-drawn curtains and the loveseat to which Jim claimed ownership. Relaxed as she seemed to an outside eye, as she readjusted her red

Ohio State throw blanket to cover up her left foot (that had kicked reflexively when Jim opened the door); as comfortable as she seemed, her stomach was tense and churning. Her grip had tightened around the stem of her wine glass, and she nibbled at the inside of her lip.

The virtually empty bottle of Merlot swished as she dragged it from the coffee table to pitch another Percocet into her dry mouth and wash it down with a single gulp of red wine. The draft from the door blew gently at the curtains, letting in enough dusty light to catch the wave of angst splashed across on her face.

Ashley was full of emotions. She was angry at the announcement from their dog, Shooter (a name that their son Tyler gave to his German Shepard puppy the day his mother brought him home seven distant birthdays ago) barking in the yard as Jim's white Chevy Silverado rolled up the gravel drive. She was annoyed at the sound of Jim's black leather dress shoes growing louder as they marched across the porch to the door. She was agitated, flexing her jaw at the tone of Jim's voice as he wrestled with his shoes in the dimly lit entrance. Finally, she was afraid, deep down, inside-her-chest afraid, as she held down the "volume up" button on the warm, slippery remote that she just realized she was strangling.

"Turn it down or turn it off!" Jim shouted as he peeled off his fancy new shoes. "My head's been pounding since noon." He spoke to the wall as he hung up the only welcome his children gave him, the only evidence of their existence this evening was their clutter piled high right in front of the door. He sighed, tickling his neatly trimmed mustache as he arched off his favorite black blazer (he told his girls that it makes him feel like one of the "men in black") and placed it on the coat rack between Tyler's letterman jacket and Ally's fur-lined, hooded coat.

Ashley shook her head. "Angry, again. *Great*. You leave those kids alone, tonight." She mumbled as Jim cocked his head to hear her, squeezing his bitter brows together and dismissing her demand like a tyrant to his oppressed.

He pressed his hands against the wall and bowed his balding salt and pepper head, finding the strength for self-control and trying to ignore the echo of Chris Harrison's dramatic line, "Ladies, this is the final rose tonight," drumming at his temples from the TV behind him. He tried counting out loud to ten, a technique he learned as a kid when he would count his father's goats as they were put into the barn for the night. He discovered it to be relaxing, calming... focusing on the number instead of the fear of a belt whipping from his father if he left one out for the coyotes to kill. Often, he would use this technique when he needed to refocus and calm down.

But today he didn't give it much of a chance. With a loud, deep sigh, he turned toward Ashley. *Hell with it*, he thought. There was rage on his face. There was tension in his chest. His Glock 9mm was bulging from his right hip and tucked firmly into his department-issued holster just a few inches behind his pocket. His detective's badge in front of his pistol gleamed from the flickering of *The Bachelor's* dramatic build-up as he crossed into the open walkway between the living room and front hall. His strides were stretched and powerful, agile and quick, balanced and athletic against the creaking of the hardwood floor. He walked heavy heeled with a soft spring from his toes, reminiscent of his old track and field running days, chasing down the leader at the state qualifying 1600-meter run. Back then he understood pain. He respected it. He craved it. He used it to release his own mental torture, his own burning agony of a fractured reality. Back then he was more of a hero than he is today.

His mouth was tight and stern. His eyes – dark and small. His hands were solid fists, scarred across the knuckles. His hate was heavy, and Ashley could feel its smothering heat getting closer.

Ashley had come to expect the hate. She lived with it all around her. Hate from her three kids, all in their teens and rebellious. Hate from her friends for not leaving the man that she called her husband. Hate from her neighbors for the shouting and burnout tires, slinging gravel at all hours of the night. She could even feel the hate from her dog for not putting up a fight when Jim forced her to tie him up outside. But especially, she had finally accepted the daily hate from her husband. It was this hate that had fueled her drug and alcohol addiction. Now she realized that his hatred was the only emotion left that she knew was real.

"I said... turn... that... down!" He growled as he reached the couch.

Ashley snapped out of her clenched-teeth daze. She glanced at the hovering monster shouting above the volume of a blonde haired Lacy desperately confessing her love to a sharp dressed Ryan. She clutched the remote, searching for that familiar power button. But the remote was slick with perspiration. It slipped from her hands and landed with a sharp rattle onto the dark, hardwood floor.

Her eyes opened from their misty, bloodshot slivers as she gazed up to a lumbering maniac firing a day's worth of anger from his thunderstorm eyes. His dark, demon figure blocked out the warm embrace of Lacy and Ryan after she had accepted his final rose.

For Ashley, time slowed down. Jim pivoted and cocked his hips. He was prepared to take a swing. His broad shoulders rotated as he raised his opened hand toward the shadows flashing on the ceiling. And with a snap of his wrist, like a bullwhip, he landed a loud hand on the top of her healing bruise.

All at once, the pain came back. Her glass of wine flung from her hand. The lamp and wine bottle crashed down onto the remote control, striking the power from the TV, leaving the two of them in near darkness. There was a soft silence, a short gust of comfort at not seeing or feeling him there anymore.

Then, came the ticking of the clock in the hallway... the excited bark of Shooter tied to an old oak tree in the yard. The room started to spin. She felt faint, dizzy. Then, there was a frustrated huff in front of her. Then another. And another. Louder. Louder. He shifted his weight forward on the creaking floor. She could smell his sour breath, she could feel his heat, his fire.

His evil whisper erected the hairs on her arms.

"Don't test me! Not today, Ashley!"

It was the last thing she heard before it all faded to black.

. . . . .

"I think Dad's home," Tyler said just loud enough for his older sister to hear across the hall in her room.

Tyler was upstairs, relaxed on his bed, bouncing a tennis ball off the wall and catching it. He had his favorite song, "Whatever it Takes" by Imagine Dragons, playing on his phone. He stroked his *barely-there* hair on his upper lip, deep in thought. His school therapist had given him the tennis ball a few months ago. Tyler recalled standing outside his door, nervously playing with his dirty blond hair just behind his ear, a habit he learned years ago while waiting for his father to get home. He laughed to himself about how he had to literally talk himself into reaching out his arm and knocking on Mike's door. He was proud of himself for not turning around and walking away.

He still thought about that day and how much he had changed since then. Mike, a tall, black man with a short graying beard, chuckled to himself for jumping at the sound of Tyler's heavy knock.

"Yes?" His deep voice rattled through the door, filling Tyler with a second wave of hesitation.

"Someone there?" Mike closed his laptop, walked to the door and swung it open, hoping to catch the prankster that knocked and ran.

"Oh! Hey, Tyler. I wasn't sure if anyone was there or not." He said, surprised.

Tyler looked up at Mike's tall, smiling face, inviting him into his office.

"Hey, Mike... uh, you got a second?"

"Sure, come on in. Have a seat."

Mike offered Tyler the purple chair in front of his desk. Tyler's face was priceless, just like many of the other males to enter Mike's office, they looked at his purple chair as if it were Barbie dolls, glitter, or a pink hula-hoop.

"What's on your mind?"

Tyler's growing athletic frame fit awkwardly into the deep purple armchair. Indeed, it was a chair that was a common joke for Mike to endure. It took some encouragement and probing questions, but Tyler eventually told him about the panic attacks he got before football games. He explained the sick, empty pit in his stomach that seemed to devour his insides in one big terrifying gulp. He described the intense burst of heat that caused his heart to thud hard at his sternum. Tyler confessed that many evenings, just before his father got home, he would get a pain in his chest and had to struggle to catch his breath. Often, he could even feel his body trembling.

They talked for his entire lunch period. Mike couldn't jot down his notes quick enough, once he got Tyler to open up. It was as if Tyler kept his emotions locked up tight inside of some safe deep in the back of his mind. Mike could sense how guarded he was. Afterward, they agreed to talk at least once a week during lunch, and Mike even got Tyler to smile on the way out the door when he said, "See ya later, Chatterbox."

It was that next session when Mike tossed him that tennis ball and told him to "squeeze the hell out of it the next time you start to feel anxious." Tyler tried to crush it in his hand when Mike asked him about his relationship with his father.

"Ally! Hey, Ally!"

Tyler threw the ball across the hallway at his sister who was laying comfortably reading her new book on her black sheeted and pillow covered bed. The ball bounced hard off her book, then her bed, and her nightstand, jingling her month-old set of keys, before bouncing across some of her drawings scattered over her desk and rolling underneath.

Her shoulders and book dropped. "What? What do you want, douchebag?"

"Could you get my ball?" Tyler grinned.

Ally's disgusted face made him laugh.

"C'mon, please?"

"Get it yourself. You threw it." Ally slid her long black hair behind her ear, picked up the book from her lap, leafed through the pages, adjusted her head back onto the pillow and kept reading.

Nikki peeked her bright head out of her room down the hall. She could hear her older brother and sister talking and wondered what it was about. To her, Ally was her idol, and Tyler was her protector. Her blonde hair was pulled back into the ponytail that she had convinced Ally into doing in exchange for a week's worth of taking out the trash. She wanted to investigate.

She held onto her diary, trying to save the page as she tip-toed down the hall and into Ally's room.

"What do you want?" Ally asked bluntly, laying her book down with an exaggerated huff.

"What are you guys talking about?" She asked, feeling left out.

"Nothin'." Ally said coldly.

"Well, I think I heard dad." Nikki's eyes were big, looking for help, for comfort, or some sort of solution to a problem.

"Yeah, so?" Ally asked, obviously annoyed.

"Hey, Nikki!" Tyler called from across the hall, now with his music low in the background. "Will you get my tennis ball? Ally's being a bitch. A big, fat bitch. Who smells bad. And who no one likes. Because she's ugly." He laughed.

"Shut up!" Being the eldest, Ally used to be able to push her brother and sister around. But now Tyler at fifteen was football big and weight-room strong. She didn't have the same pull as she used to. So, she just took it out on Nikki.

"Aren't you supposed to be doing your homework?" Ally shot at Tyler.

Tyler looked down at the pile of papers and notebooks on the floor beside his bed. "Maybe!" He yelled.

Nikki's eyes were shifting around the room looking for Tyler's ball as her brother and sister did their usual *back and forth*.

"It's over there, Nikki. Under my desk." Ally motioned in that direction. "And don't knock anything off!"

Nikki walked carefully over to Ally's desk. Her big sister's colored pencils were scattered across a new drawing that Nikki hadn't seen before. Ally, being the artist of the family, would usually show *everyone* in the house her latest work. One day, Tyler explained to Nikki that it was just her way to gloat, to brag, or to get the attention that she lacked and clearly needed. But Nikki defended her. Nikki thought her work was amazing and loved to see it. She expressed to Tyler that Ally had something to be proud of, and she loved when Ally would share her drawings. Tyler had just smirked, playfully messed up his little sister's hair, and laughed at how naive she was.

Nikki started to reach for the drawing on the desk.

"What's this?" Nikki asked. "A new drawing?"

Ally shot up in bed. "Don't touch that!"

Nikki's hand jerked back as if it had scraped against a hot stove.

"I'm not," Nikki said innocently. "I just wanted to see it."

"Well, it's not done."

"I don't care. I love your artwork, Ally." Nikki was standing cautiously at her desk pleading her case with sad eyes.

"Why?"

"Because you're amazing! That's why."

Ally set her book down and stared at Nikki's honest face. She deeply desired to share her work, but compliments from her little sister weren't as meaningful as those from her mother and father.

Ally was especially proud of this one. She had drawn it from a dream she had a few nights ago. In her dream, she could see her father standing in the doorway to Nikki's room surrounded by a black haze. Nikki was asleep in her bed. There was a light coming from her room. Suddenly, Ally became her father. There was a rush of emotions coursing through her mind. She felt ashamed, dirty, embarrassed, angry, and mean. Then, she looked down at her father's hands and saw that they were covered in blood. Panic and fury woke her up in a cold, breathless sweat. The next morning, she started to draw that scene.

"Go ahead, look at it. Whatever. I don't care." Ally picked up her book and pretended to be reading again as she watched her sister's face from over the top of the pages.

Nikki scraped and rolled away the colored pencils revealing the blood-soaked hands outside her room. She gasped.

"Ally, is this me? Is this *my* room? Is that *Dad?*"

"Yeah, so what?"

Nikki picked up the picture and admired it. It was beautiful. It was terrifying. It was real.

"I love it. But it scares me." Nikki sat it back down and covered it up with a notebook.

"Thanks," Ally muttered, a smile creeping at her lips.

Satisfied, Nikki bent to her hands and knees and crawled halfway under the desk, stretching out to grab the ball that had rolled between the back of the desk and wall.

The slow, familiar thud of Jim's heavy steps creaking down the hallway made her freeze.

What kind of day is he having? Is he in a good mood? A bad mood? Is he tired? I hope he's tired. Her panicked thoughts tore at her fragile state of mind. She knew that she was in the wrong position if her father walked through the door. She tried to back out quickly but smacked her head on the edge of the desk. The sudden pain stopped her in her tracks.

Jim's appearance in the doorway, arms crossed and leaning against the doorframe, cast a towering shadow that consumed Nikki's body as she rubbed her aching head. *Shit.* She thought.

"What are you two lovely ladies doing?" He asked. His attention bringing a faint smile to Ally's face as she searched his for recognition.

But Jim's eyes were fixed on Nikki. Ally watched as he sucked in her adolescent form, his eyes growing softer as she struggled to exit that small space. Ally's jealousy turned to disgust as she witnessed his eyes studying Nikki's rear as she wiggled from the desk.

She squeezed out the frustration in her jaw and shook her head. She knew exactly what kind of night it was going to be.

"Need some help, Nik?" Jim asked as if they were best buddies. "Need a hand?"

"No, no that's ok, Dad. I got it." She gathered herself to her feet, still rubbing the back of her head and now holding onto Tyler's tennis ball.

Jim laughed. "Well look at you all grown up and independent. Before long, I'll be fighting off the boys with a stick."

That comment made all three of his children cringe.

Tyler paused the music on his phone, "Maybe some catch before dark?" He asked trying to change the subject.

Jim inhaled, paused, and then released it noisily. "Not tonight, Ty. It's been a long day."

Tyler shrugged, satisfied at breaking his attention.

Ally perked with the chance to relate to her father.

"Yeah, me too! You should hear about the day I had, Dad... first–"

"Not now Ally," he interrupted. "Just let me gather my thoughts. I have a lot on my mind, right now."

This crushed her. She fell to pieces on her bed, sinking into the pillows and out of existence. But no one noticed, *he* didn't notice.

Instead, his head was bent, and he was rubbing his temples with his left hand. He sighed, shifted his weight to the other foot and looked up at Nikki. His right hand could be heard tapping onto the grip of his pistol.

"Nik, can I talk to you about something here in a bit?" He sounded so casual, so friendly, so endearing. His voice was soft and pitched... gentle, even. A tone that they all had come dangerously to know meant quite the opposite.

Nikki took half a step back, instinctually, unintentionally. "We can talk right now if you want? Ally won't mind. Will you Ally?" She asked in desperation.

Jim frowned. He seemed to take offense to Nikki's reaction. "No, Nichole. We will have our discussion here in a bit, in my room, like always." His features turned from soft to hard, from light to dark, from fatherly to demonic.

Just as instantly as he appeared, he left, strutting away toward his room, loosening his tie and unfastening his belt.

Nikki looked up from the ground and met Ally's stare. They held each other's gaze for a moment, each understanding the other. Nikki looked out the window, to the tree branches that nearly reached the window's edge. Ally's eyes followed. Nikki thought to run, to escape into the black distance. Maybe she could make it to Trisha's house, or even Mrs. V's, which was just a few miles into town.

Ally watched her younger sister, who would be twelve years old soon, question her entire existence. She watched her face turn from despair, to shame, to indignation. She knew her face, her rage, her storm. She understood what she was thinking, because she had been there before, and she watched as Nikki contemplated her escape into the moonlight.

Ally hung her head, studying her forearm, tracing her own faded scars. Each line an attempt to understand, a jagged effort to let out the pain. Each lingering, red slash an attempt to escape so long ago.

She shivered and yanked her sleeve down a little further. Her eyes softened as she reached out and grabbed Nikki's hand.

Her voice was at a whisper. "Nik, it'll be ok."

She tugged on her arm and stroked Nikki's hand with her thumb.

"Do you hear me? We can get through this." She said a little louder, more convincing this time.

Tyler's presence at the door dimmed the hallway light. He stood just inside the doorway, flexing with rage, his arms bulging in his cut-off t-shirt and mesh shorts. They both looked up at him, startled by his magnitude.

His stone eyes fixed on Nikki – his voice eager and bold.

"I have a plan."

Nikki's eyes darted up from his chest. Ally snapped and cocked her head.

"A plan?" Ally questioned. "Seriously?"

Her sarcasm was easy to read.

He crossed his arms. "Yeah. A plan. Look, I've been doing a lot thinking, lately... and I think the only way that we're going to get through this is... well... to get rid of... *him*," he motioned his head toward his father's room, "I think that we have to do something about it ourselves. You know? Take charge, create our own destiny, grab the bull by the horns and all that other shit."

He looked at the both of them, Nikki nodding her head and at Ally's scrunched up skeptical face.

"I'm serious, Ally."

Tyler and his older sister had always been in competition with one another. Tyler thought that he was the smart one and Ally saw him as the dumb jock. Ally had the gift of imagination, and she wasn't afraid to show it. Especially, when Tyler would invite his friends over to play football in the yard. Ally wasn't much in stature, a slender frame, more elegant than athletic, more princess than anything, as her dad used to call her. But at sixteen, she had already figured out how to work the boys. She would lay out sunbathing while Tyler and his friends played football in the yard. She knew what she was doing, flipping out her towel just close enough to be a distraction and just far enough away to make them more concerned about her two-piece than the football game. Honestly, those boys didn't stand a chance. Even when Tyler called her out on it, even after he whined that it was *his* time to hang out with his buddies, she would be out there on a towel in her hot pink bikini top and rubbing on oil for all the boys to see. That was how she filled the void from her father's attention, which had shifted to Nikki a few years ago. She knew what she was doing, and she loved it.

Nikki plopped onto the bed beside Ally. Ally may have been more skeptical, but Nikki was analyzing different strategies in her head. *Call the cops, run away, run him over with Ally's car....*

"What *kind* of plan?"

Shutting it behind him gently, Tyler sat in the rolling chair at Ally's desk. He spun around a couple of times playfully, before readjusting himself in front of his sister's latest drawing: a beautiful blooming rose with a thorny stem and three fallen petals. He felt out of place. Looking around, he tried to remember the last time that he had actually *sat down* in her room. It always made him feel uncomfortable, *Too much girl*, he would tell her: a poster of a shirtless male model's six-pack abs, one of Justin Bieber on stage reaching out and touching the hand of a girl in the front row, which she had drawn hearts onto a couple of years ago. There were pictures, perfumes, jewelry scarfs, skirts, and shoes... so... many... shoes.

"Don't touch anything," she warned, "I don't want your *stupid* to get all over it."

Her satisfying smirk made him chuckle. He picked up the rose drawing and rubbed it all over his body, giving it a few extra strokes under his arms.

"There, now *it's* stupid, too." Grinning victory, he tossed it to the ground like he was "dropping the mic."

"Oh my God! You're so disgusting! You jerk! Get out! Just get out of my room, you nasty... barbarian."

She growled and threw her book at him. He caught it against his chest and laughed. He stood up and walked it back over to her and squeezing it tightly when she tried to yank it from his hand, before letting go on her third try and sending her falling back into the pillows.

He raised his hands as if he did nothing wrong. "Alright. That's fine. I'll go. No problem."

"Wait! Wait!" Nikki and Ally both begged.

"Let's hear this *plan.*" Ally grabbed a pillow, sat up and leaned over it in her lap.

Nikki reached out and pulled at Tyler's arm.

"Don't leave. Please. Tell us your plan. Tell us how to get rid of... dad." Her head dropped. Her voice was desperate. "I'll do anything, Ty... *anything.*"

As the baby sister, Nikki felt left out. Being a few years younger, she still had some growing up to do. She still played with dolls, even though Ally would tease her. She kind of liked the attention from her big sister, but sometimes she was just mean. So, instead of telling Ally or her mom her secrets, she started writing them down in a diary. In short stories and philosophical essays, she would open up about the ugliness of her family, about the lies that they would tell in public, but mostly about the confusion and anger swelling inside of her. Recently, after studying Wolfe and Joyce, she started scribbling poems in her diary. She was a natural poet, great at describing imagery and emotion through words. She wrote poems that would incite turbulence and tears in the reader. They were strong worded confessionals that brought the reader to understand her chaos and rage when her father forced her to touch him.

Tyler knelt to his knee in front of the bed, eye level with Ally. Nikki mimicked her older brother. "Alright, but listen... if this is going to work, if we're actually going to pull this off, then we can't tell anyone. I mean it. Nobody can know. Not mom. Not your friends, not even Brian. Got it?"

He stared at Ally waiting for her response. She just rolled her eyes and looked at Nikki.

"I mean it, Ally. We could... well, we could go to *jail* for this."

"Jesus, what kind of plan are we talking about, here, murder!?"

Nikki's big blue eyes snapped toward her sister's lips.

"Murder? I don't want to go to prison!" Nikki looked back and forth between both of them. "But, anything would be better than... his room."

Silence set in as all three of them thought about consequences that came with *getting rid of their father.* Ally brushed her wild hair behind her ear and looked out the window to her left. The leaves were dead or dying. Winter was coming, and the bright colors of fall were fading to brown and gray. The wind gently swayed the maple tree not too far from her window. She watched a yellow leaf, twirl, and glide gently to the ground.

"Look, we're not seriously talking about... *killing* dad, are we?!"

Tyler was quick to argue his point with wild, exaggerated hands and a low, yelling whisper.

"Well, what the hell do you suggest?! I mean, c'mon! We've all seen what he's capable of... we've all seen how much *help* 'the system' is. What choice do we have left? What else is there to do?"

Nikki put her hand on Ally's arm. Ally could feel it trembling, or maybe it was *her* arm that was shaking, she wasn't sure, but she looked down at it, and then up at her.

"Ally, I don't know how much longer I can do this. I've tried to be strong, but I'm not like you, I can't just *bury it* and move on."

"Bury it!? You think that's what I did? Seriously?! There's not a day that goes by where I don't see him on top of me! His eyes so dark and hollow, his breath heavy, his... There's–" Ally started to break down. Her eyes filled with tears. She wiped at them with her sleeve before they made it to her chin. "I just want him to love me!"

Nikki started to cry, too. "I just want him *gone*, like before. Ally, he's not our dad anymore. He's not! He's a monster!"

Tyler, still on his knee, reached out toward the bed, toward his sisters, placing his hand beside them, not too close, but just close enough to let them know that he felt their pain. He bent his head into his other hand. Although it had been years since his father had molested him, the pain was still sharp. There wasn't anything that bonded these children together like the torment that they all tolerated and shared from their father.

He looked up at his sisters with *"I've had enough"* burning in his eyes.

"What else are we going to do? You want to run away, again? You want to see how far you can run from a homicide detective?" He gave a short, winded laugh. "They'll just find you, again... bring you back here, again... all smiles, all happy... thinking that they have done something good... claiming victory, not knowing that they just condemned us all to Hell."

"But he's our father!" She was sturdy, solid, and certain. She looked at Nikki for help and then at Tyler. "He's our... dad," She trailed off, defeated, fighting with the fantasy of what she always wished he *would be*: the father that she would tell her secrets to, the father that she would come to for advice, a father that she would look up to. *That* type of dad. The type of man that she would hope to marry someday, raise a family with, love, honor, and cherish. But, deep down inside, despite all of her *daddy issues,* her craving for his love and attention... she knew that he wasn't **that** kind of man. She knew that he could *never be* that type of man.

She bit her lower lip, realized that she was holding her breath and let it go. "Alright, what's the plan?"

• • • • •

Nikki understood that she was the bait. She understood that she had to be strong. Unlike her sister, she refused to bury the pain. She wasn't that type. Even when she was younger, she would face her fears head-on. Much like the situation a few years ago, when a pit bull came trotting out of the tree line and into the yard while she was playing fetch with Shooter. Shooter growled as it got close. Then the pit bull attacked. Nikki watched in horror as the two dogs snapped at each other, each one biting the other. Then, Shooter's back leg gave out, the bad one, the one that Jim had broken when Shooter showed his teeth trying to defend Ashley from Jim's heavy hand. Nikki knew that she had to do something. Shooter was on his back, and the pit bull was on top of him. She looked around and grabbed a heavy stick. Then she ran at them, screaming as loud as she could, swinging the stick wildly. It was just enough distraction for Shooter to regain control and send the pit bull, bloodied, back to wherever he came from.

A couple of weeks had passed since they discussed the plan. There were several second thoughts, evenings of talking it out, of planning and coordinating together. It had turned into a couple of weeks of bonding and understanding that *this* was the only way. They had to do what so many others had failed to do. They had to stop this evil from walking the earth. They had to exterminate this filth, this vile existence of a man claiming to be their "father." But a father, a dad, a *man*, does not destroy a family as Jim had. Instead, they considered him less than blood, less than flesh, less than heart and soul. No, they no longer saw Jim as their father, but as a pest, a tick sucking the life from them, a flea spreading Black Death among them. He was hate, and they were love. And their intentions were to destroy him.

Jim was sipping on his third Jim Beam and Coke, which Ally had poured for him. It was a little on the heavy side, but he didn't seem to mind. (On good days, he would joke that his family invented Jim Beam, naming it after his great grandfather, so he was entitled to drink as much and as often as he wanted.) He was watching NCIS in *his* chair while Ashley cleaned up the dishes in the kitchen. It had been a pretty decent couple of days. There had been no fighting, no arguing, no apparent evil lurking around in the shadows. For now, the Devil was at bay and Ally wanted to call it off, suggesting that maybe he had changed. On those particularly optimistic days, she clung tightly to hope. But Nikki and Tyler convinced her that it was time to face their demons. It was time to take back their lives.

"Dad," Nikki said, stepping through the walkway into the living room, "I'm... I'm ready for our *talk*."

"What? Oh, yeah." Jim looked at his shiny silver watch. It was just after 8 p.m., "I guess it is getting a little late." He ran his hand along his thigh and back up again to his crotch, adjusting himself. "Yeah, we should probably do it before it gets much later." He downed the last of his Jim Beam and groaned out of his love seat recliner. "Let's go," was all he said as he passed her and headed up the steps.

Ashley watched from over her shoulder as he led Nikki up to their bedroom. She hadn't taken any pills today and had simply enjoyed one glass of wine for dinner. She was aware of Nikki's fate but didn't know how to stop it. Jim had beat her bloody the last time she had confronted him about what was happening to her children. So, she just watched with disgust, with sadness, and with weakness as that son of a bitch led her daughter by the hand, up the steps, and into the bed that they still shared.

Nikki gave Tyler and Ally a quick look as she passed by their opened and waiting bedroom doors. They were pretending to watch TV, anxiously waiting for them to walk by. As soon as they did, Tyler looked at Ally, held up two fingers and mouthed "two minutes" across the hall. She let out a heavy sigh and closed her eyes. She was still holding onto something, still battling right and wrong. Deep down inside of her, she still wanted her father back. But, she could see the death inside of Nikki's eyes, and despite their differences, she had an aching to protect her younger sister.

Jim shut the door and turned on the nightstand light.

"So, how's school going?" He asked nonchalantly as he took off his shirt. This cycle of abuse had become so normal to him, now, that he was comfortable enough to engage in small talk. Of course, it wasn't always that way. The first several times Nikki kicked and punched. But she surrendered after he squeezed her throat and threatened to pull the life right out of her.

Nikki stood there watching her father undress down to his boxer briefs, stalling, hoping that her brother and sister would rescue her soon.

"It was okay, how was your day?" She hoped conversation would stall his intentions.

Jim chuckled, almost as evil, almost as empty as the act that he was so eager to commit.

"Fine, I guess. Now, come over here. Sit down." He lowered himself to the bed and pat the comforter beside him.

Nikki walked slowly, still stalling, still burning the seconds away.

"Come on, I don't have all night. Take off your shirt." His words were slightly slurred.

Nikki slid off her shirt, leaving on her bra, and sat down beside her father. He ran his hand across her shoulder and then up her neck.

"You're starting to grow up, you know," he said casually. "Soon, you'll be a woman. Soon, I won't have much use for you." His words seemed more like thoughts spoken out loud than conversation.

She ignored him, sitting on the bed shirtless as her father ran his hand over her body. She closed her eyes and tried to take herself away from his rough hands and whiskey breath. Her breathing became deep and controlled. She focused on her chest moving in and out, on her shoulders rising and falling. In her mind, she counted after each gasp, watched as the numbers faded into existence in her head. She felt them. She created them. She became them.

It was one of the few precious things that she had learned from her father before he set out to ravish her. It was a generous gift he gave her, the day that she had walked in on Ally cutting her forearms. She had nightmares for days after seeing her sister's blood. One night, after waking up the entire house while screaming herself awake, Jim told her that he had a secret to share about how he would calm himself down after nightmares when he was a kid.

He leaned down close to her ear to whisper. "Just close your eyes. Think of somewhere happy and safe. Breathe in slow and deep. Count slowly to ten and then back down again, if you have to." It was a technique that she had mastered by now.

"I wonder what I'll do once you're a little older." He was definitely thinking out loud now. "I suppose I'll just have to find someone else to love as much as you."

His words pierced her concentration, and she cringed at the thought of someone else facing this torture. She sucked in air loudly through her nose, tried to find her strength, and started counting again.

He stood up and slid off his underwear.

"Go ahead." He motioned, standing in front of her.

Ally was on her way back up the stairs with another strong drink for her father. Tyler was searching through his sock drawer for the bottle of Percocet he swiped from his mother's purse last night.

Ally rounded the corner into Tyler's room.

"Hurry," he said, "she can't stall forever."

He ripped open the pills and poured them all into the Jim Beam. Ally swirled the drink with her finger, letting them dissolve.

"C'mon... c'mon." Tyler encouraged until they fizzled out and blended with the amber drink. Tyler looked at Ally and nodded.

"Ready? Let's do this." Tyler handed her the glass. "Remember, act normal."

She started down the hallway, careful not to spill any of the poison. Tyler was right behind her holding onto her shoulder for comfort.

She knocked on her father's door.

Jim was pulling his daughter's pants to the ground.

"Not now!" he shouted from the other side.

"I brought you another drink." Ally offered innocently.

Jim yanked off Nikki's pants and tossed them into the corner.

"Just leave it!" He yelled back, his words obviously slurring.

"Okay." Ally set the glass in front of the door, splashing some over the rim and onto the hardwood floor. *Crap.* She thought, wiping at it with her bare hand.

Then, they both hurried carefully back to Tyler's room. Wide-eyed, they stared at each other for a moment and then peered around the door frame, waiting for their father to consume his fate.

Jim opened the door bare naked.

Ally and Tyler jumped back into the room, tripping over each other and bumping into the dresser, knocking over some of Tyler's football trophies.

Jim didn't notice. He was too focused on his drink, on his pleasure.

"Shh." Ally held her finger up to her lips.

Tyler set the trophies back onto the dresser, quietly. Ally crawled up to the door, barely poking her compact mirror out just far enough to see what was happening.

Jim stood in the black mass pouring out from behind him into the hallway light. He glanced around, grunted, and bent down to grab his drink. He stumbled, caught himself, rebalanced and reached down, again. This time he steadied himself on the wall. He wrapped his fingers around it firmly, felt its cold dampness, smelled the sweetness of alcohol and a splash of coke as he pulled it up to his lips, the ice clinked against the glass. He stood there in the doorway – darkness behind him, light in front. He took a lingering sweet swallow and turned and headed back into the shadows.

"Jim! Jim you bastard! You God damned bastard!"

Ally and Tyler snapped their heads toward each other and froze, eyes wide with shock, with fear.

Jim's shoulder slouched. He turned around annoyed, letting his drink dangle to his side.

His wife stood firm at the top of the stairs, like that old oak in the yard that outlasted last year's windstorm. Her arms were extended, Jim's duty pistol squeezed into her hands, her finger shaking on the trigger.

"I won't let you hurt us anymore! You hear me? You're done! You're through!" Her eyes narrowed as she pointed the pistol at Jim's thumping heart. "Now go to Hell!"

Shocked and startled to be staring down the barrel of his own Glock, he let the Jim Beam slip from his hand. It fell, wet and loud, splashing and shattering across the hardwood floor.

TWO.
NIKKI

One year earlier
2017, October

Music. That's what makes me happy. All kinds, really, and... don't tell mom... *or Ally*, but sometimes I listen to music that I'm not supposed to, like, Rihanna, Kesha, and Alessia Cara. Oh, my God, her song, *Scars To Your Beautiful,* is **the best!** It really gets me right in the feels. I like songs like that. You know, the ones that you can relate to and stuff. Or rap, cause, well... it makes me want to get up and shake my booty! You knooow... yes, you do. You know what I'm talking about. Don't lie.

Ally says that I don't have a booty. But, neither does she... so whatever. Anyway, I like to sneak into her room and listen to her music when she's out with Brian, or whatever. I just log onto her computer. *I know the password.* It wasn't that hard to figure out... *Daddyslittlegirl. Yeah, it doesn't take a genius to figure that one out.* She's been telling me forever that she was "Daddy's little girl" first! She says that Dad gives me more attention just because I'm the baby of the family. She says not to feel special, because "every baby of the family" gets spoiled like I do. She says that I'm not *that* special. Whatever. Tyler says that Ally is just being a... a *B-word* and not to worry about anything she says, because I *am* special. He says that I'm the most special eleven-year-old (my birthday was last week) that he's ever met. You know what I think? I think Tyler is just trying to be a big brother. Big brothers *have* to say stuff like that. Right?

School's great! I actually really like it! Everyone said that sixth grade would be scary, but after the first week, it was just like every other grade. We go to class, we raise our hand, we do homework, we take tests, and then we get graded. I'm getting all A's and B's, by the way...*aaand* I have like, a ninety-eight percent in Language Arts. Mostly because I love to write. But, also, because I totally like Mrs. V. She's so nice, funny, and easy to talk to. She makes us write in our journal for five minutes at the beginning of every class. I love it. I get to write about whatever I want. Or, if I'm stuck, Mrs. V. puts a prompt up on the board and we can write about that if we want. Sometimes, when I write something *really* awesome, I just *haaave* to bring it home and read it to mom. She'll let me sit on the floor in front of her, and she brushes my hair while she watches one of those silly dating shows. Mom says that I get it from her and that she's so proud of me. She used to be a writer... or, well... she *is* a writer. I'm not sure if you ever stop being one once you start. She even had a book published! It's called, *A Tale of Love and War*. It's about two lovers who struggle to stay together. First, they love each other then, they hate each other... but by the end, they're head over heels in love, again. That's why I'll never fall in love. It just sounds crazy to me. But, Mom won't let me read it. She says that it's not appropriate for my age. Whatever. She doesn't know that I listen to Drake (He's a hottie!). So, what? They're just curse words. Seriously, it's like Tyler says, it's not that big of a deal.

My friends? Well, I can't think of anyone that I'm *not* friends with. Well, except for Trisha. She's just unfriendable. She's too big to a sixth grader, with her shaggy brown hair and freckles. She calls me Goldie Locks, but not in a friendly way. I think she also steals my pens... but, I can't prove it. She picks on *eeeveryone*. Mrs. V. told me that's just what bullies do. She thinks I should give her a chance, though, for like... the hundredth time. She explained that a lot of times, bullies are just hurting inside and that Trisha probably just needs a friend. I said, "like that stray cat that digs in the dumpster in the parking lot and hisses at you whenever you try to pet it?" I'm always able to make Mrs. V. laugh. *Sheee,* thinks I'm special.

But, I decided to take her advice a few weeks ago at lunch. It was pizza day, which of course is my favorite. I did a victory lap around the couch when Dad gave me extra money to buy an extra slice of pizza, because, "I'm extra amazing." Ally didn't appreciate my pizza dance. She's such a lame-o.

When I finally made it to the cafeteria, the lunch line was long, like, all-the-way-down-the-hall-by-the-gym-door, long. There were already kids getting in line for "seconds." I stayed after class to run my plan by Mrs. V. because I was second guessing myself. But, she approved, and her smile was encouraging. She even wished me luck as I ran out the door.

The lunchroom was loud. A bunch of excited pizza-face kids. My stomach wasn't happy that I took forever. It smelled so good, and the noise was so big that I had a hard time listening to my thoughts as I practiced what I would say to Trisha. *Hey, Trisha. I'm Nikki. How's your day going? No. Hey, Trish. I really like your shirt. C'mooon. Trish, (wink and point) heeey, remember me? You going to the dance this Friday? You're lookin' pretty snazzy, today. What's the special occasion? Hey Trish, Trish... buddy... friend... pal... bully.* I wasn't really sure what to say to a mean girl. Does a bully *like* to be called bully? I don't know. Whatever.

Instead, I figured I'd let my food do the talking. The lunch lady looked me up and down when I asked for three slices.

"But, you're just a tiny thing." She said, with greasy spatula frozen in the air.

"Won't be for long if you keep eating like that," said her hairnetted sidekick.

"Oh, it's not all for me, I'm getting a slice for my... *friend-bully*." My arms were getting tired from holding out my tray.

"That's very sweet of you, darlin'." She winked as she flopped two more slices in a messy stack on top of each other.

I walked out of the line with a smile that I could hardly contain. I was *enthu... enthudiass... nooo, I was... enthusiastic!* (We learned that word last week in Language Arts. I told Mrs. V. that I was going to use it sometime.)

Anyway, I paused and searched for her in the back of the cafeteria. *That's where the kids without many friends sit.* There were only a handful of empty or nearly empty tables, and well, she's not a small girl, so it wasn't that hard to find her. Wait, is that mean? I'm just saying... ugh, never mind. Sorry. Anyway, my friends kept calling out my name, thinking I was lost or something when I walked right past our usual table in the front and headed straight for the back.

Trisha had her back to the crowd, stuffing her face. I couldn't blame her. I mean, I ate *three pepperonis* just on the way to her table. She didn't see me freeze behind her in a moment of panic. (Thank God for that. I'm sure she would've made fun of me.) Then, one deep breath and a reminder that *sometimes a bully just needs a friend.*

"Hey, Trish... *aaa*." I stuttered like a moron. *(Nailed it!)*

She didn't budge from her tray of pizza and two bags of chips.

So, I walked a little closer and moved to the side of her, so she could see me.

"Trisha. Hey. It's me... I'm Nikki. Nikki Handler. We go to school together." *Idiot.*

With her mouth full and a quick head snap in my direction, she glared at me, trying to figure out why I was disturbing her meal.

"What do you want, Goldie Locks?"

"Can I..." I swallowed that choking feeling in my throat.

She was already going back for another bite.

"Can you **what?**"

I could feel the stares of egg-eyed sixth graders burning into my back of my orange "Colt Pride" t-shirt. The few tables around us fell silent. They were waiting for her to devour me. I just stood there beside her and her empty table, probably looking pale and parched as my stomach growled, *Feed me! Feed me!* It was now or never. I straightened up, locked my knees in place and clenched my tray like a shield protecting me from her laser beam glares.

I smiled with fear in my eyes. "Can I sit with you, today?"

She stopped chewing and whipped my way, again. She studied me, looking for any cracks, for the punch line, for any signs of a junior high joke.

"*Why?*"

"I don't know... you don't have anyone to sit with. I just thought I would..."

"What makes you think that I don't have anyone to sit with?" She was glaring at me, not giving an inch.

I looked around at all five empty chairs, at all five empty spaces. Then, I looked at the almost empty tables around us, pizza halfcocked to their mouths, all staring at our showdown.

I slobbered over my tray, smelling the melted cheese and two pepperonis left. *I wasn't about to eat cold pizza!*

"Well, I'm sitting, a*nd*, I brought you an extra slice." I pulled out a chair, not the one directly beside her, but the next chair after that.

Her eyes were still hard and fixed on my face. She was still studying my angle. I slid my tray between us.

"Here, pick one. Sorry, I *kinda* ate some of the pepperonis."

She looked down at my offering, then up to my face, down at the pizza, licking her lips, and then back up at me. Her eyes softened, her defenses fell. Just like me, pizza was her kryptonite.

We ate in silence for the first few minutes, and then she did something so bizarre, sooo... awkward... so nice, that I started to feel sad for her. She *thanked me*. She said that no one had ever shared their food with her. That no one even wanted to sit next to her.

We spent the rest of the period talking about what we like to do, what we don't like to do, and that I should just call her *Trish*, and she should just call me *Nik*. She told me about her parents' divorce, how her sister lives with her mom, and that she lives with her dad. She talked me about her dad's temper, just like I was her... therapist... she told me about all the pain that he has caused her.

I felt that. You know? I felt her pain. I connected with her. In a strange, weird, funny way... I felt like I knew her.

I confessed about my dad's anger too... about how he beats mom and drinks every night.

I even showed her how I get through the pain. I shared my secret weapon, about how I had watched my father close his eyes when he was upset and count out loud over and over again until he was finally relaxed.

I showed her how to do it. How to breathe in and out, real deep, through your nose and out your mouth. I told her to count *really* slow to ten. I told her to close her eyes and imagine somewhere beautiful, somewhere happy and warm. I said that the secret to feeling better was as simple as counting to ten.

• • • • •

Dad? Yeah, I mean... he's alright. He's always buying me things... gets me anything I want. But, I don't really like to talk about him, much. He's **not** the hero that I thought he was. You know? He's a... he's a *taker*, and like Mrs. V. says, that makes him a bully. But he doesn't need a friend, he has lots of those, he needs... *Jesus*. Or Hell. I'm not really sure which. Is there any hope for him? What do you think? Do you think that Dad can... *get better*?

It's hard to talk about it. I'd rather just **write** about it. What's that word you use... theerrraaa... *peutic*? Yeah, *therapeutic*. Writing is therapeutic. It helps me organize my thoughts and release stress. I can write a poem, or a letter, or even a story about whatever is bothering me at the time. I love writing stories. I mean, in stories you can make the characters do whatever you'd like them to.

So, I wrote this story about Haley. She's this quiet girl in my Language

Arts class. I think she's shy. I talk to her sometimes, but she doesn't say much. She's totally pretty though. She has *really* blue eyes and blonde hair. She's skinny, about my height, and she bites her nails just like me.

Well anyway, Mrs. V. gave us the whole period to write about "Courage." She said that we could write about anything at all to do with courage. It didn't have to be about us, or our family, or even someone we know. I thought about writing a story about a soldier, or a cop... or even a teacher. But, everyone was writing about that. I wanted to write about Haley.

In my story, Haley is the baby of the family. They live out in the country, kind of like we do, but even further from town than us. She's not as quiet at home. She plays and laughs with her brother and sister. *She's super close to her older sister.* They're like, **best friends!** Her older brother is always taking care of her, always protecting her. She's so happy at home.

But, one day, her uncle, from West Virginia, came to stay with them for a few weeks. He had a gambling problem and lost all of his money. Well, Haley's uncle was her dad's brother, and her dad told him that he could sleep in Haley's room. Since she was the baby, she had to share a room with her older sister. But, she didn't mind, because, like I said... they were *besties*.

The first few days were weird having someone new in the house. But they all got used to it. Haley's uncle was pretty funny and always telling inappropriate jokes (I'm not going to say them out loud). They were... *dirty* jokes. Haley would laugh just to make him feel good, even if she didn't understand all of them. She enjoyed being around her uncle. But that didn't last long.

Haley's uncle was a *perv!* He would talk about her body, her bra size, and how she should lay out to get a tan because that's what the older boys like. Soon, Haley started to feel uneasy around her uncle. He didn't make her feel very comfortable anymore.

One day, Haley caught him watching her change. He said it was an accident, but she didn't think it was. She thought about telling her mom, or maybe even her dad. But she didn't want to get her uncle in trouble. Besides, they probably wouldn't believe her, anyway. So, she didn't tell anyone. She kept it a secret.

The next day, her uncle offered to babysit Haley while she was home "sick." Haley told her mom that she would be fine alone, but her mom was very worried about her and wanted someone to be there to keep an eye on her.

She even *thanked* Haley's uncle for offering to babysit.

That day, Haley's uncle put his hands up her shirt. He said that he wanted to make sure that her heart was beating right. He said he might have to take her to the hospital, if not. She didn't like that. She hated hospitals. So, she let him touch her.

But Haley's uncle didn't stop there. He touched her in more places. He even made her touch *him,* too. He said that it was to make sure that he wasn't getting sick, too. Haley and her uncle touched each other a lot that day.

When Haley's parents got home, they could tell that something was wrong. They asked a lot of questions, but Haley didn't know how to answer them. She was scared that she would get in trouble. So, she made up a story about how she threw up in the living room, and her uncle helped her clean it up. That's what she made her parents believe for a whole week.

Haley started to have dreams about her uncle touching her in the middle of the night. She was so worried and scared. She didn't know what to do. On some nights, she even cried herself to sleep.

She decided to tell her dad. Because, well... because Dad could protect her. But that's not what he did. Instead, her dad got <u>very</u> angry. He said that making up lies like that could ruin someone's life and their career.

He told Haley that she had to show him exactly what she thinks her uncle did to her. Haley tried to tell him. But he told her that she had to *show* him. He *forced her* to show him everything. So, she did. She pulled all the courage and strength from her soul, and she did everything all over again. And it changed her forever. She wanted to tell someone. She wanted to scream. Haley wanted to fight back.

It was killing her to keep everything inside. She knew that she had to say something to someone. But, she didn't know how. And she was very afraid of what everyone would think of her. She thought that she had done something wrong. She thought that she would get yelled at.

Finally, a few weeks later, after her uncle finally went back home, she had told her mom that she didn't want to be around him or dad anymore. Her mom asked a lot of questions. Haley had to be very brave, again. She answered them all so honestly. She, *finally,* told the truth, *all* of the truth.

Her mom hugged her, cried, and told her how much she loved her. Haley cried, too. The weight of carrying all that pain and worry around with her had finally been lifted. Haley could finally start to be happy, again.

She went to school and made new friends. She raised her hand to answer questions in class. She even started dating an *eighth grader!* Although she still had scars from what her dad and uncle did to her, she knew that she had the courage to move on. She knew that she could face anything because she was brave... because she was a warrior, a survivor.

That's it. That's the end.

That's my story... uh, about Haley.

THREE.
ALLY

2017, November

The truth is, I haven't always hated people. I used to love life. I used to have friends. Jessica. Jessica *was* my friend. I can still remember playing over to her house when I was, like, I don't know, seven or eight. She had this tire swing that was tied to this one rogue branch that veered off to the right, while all the others headed toward the sun, on a huge tree in her front yard. We used to push each other for what seemed like hours and talk about those idiot boys at school, our new clothes, or how our mamas liked to brush our hair. That was before mine had her... uh, *problem.*

There's no doubt I was happier back then, before all this other bullshit. Back when dad still loved me or at least acted like it. But Jessica was a good friend, as far as third-grade friendships go, beautiful, with her Taylor Swift hair, always combed with bangs. And then there was me with my always-in-a-ponytail midnight hair. We sat beside each other at lunch, and sometimes we'd share our food. I remember when Mom used to make this kickass pineapple upside down cake, and every Monday she would wrap a huge slice in tinfoil and write these cute little notes, like, *Have a wonderful day sweetie! Remember, you're just as sweet as this cake!* I loved that. And, so did Jessica, because sometimes I'd share... well, if her mom had made those delish chocolate chip cookies. Ha-ha. Even back then, I guess it was all about me.

Sometimes Jessica would come over to my house, after all, we had the best yard to go exploring in. I guess you could say that I was a bit of a tomboy, back then. No matter how often Dad would call me his little princess or "Daddy's little girl," we were still turning over every rock, stick, and piece of trash trying to find worms for the pond in the backfield. Jessica in her hand-me-down-jeans and I in my new Hollister's that mom would buy *with dad's money.* But he didn't mind. He's always spoiled us that way. Jessica didn't know how to bait her own hook so I would do it for her, just like Dad had shown me. We'd sit there on the little patch of dirt that Dad had cleared in the chest-high grass so that mom and him could see us from the back porch, while we threw rocks at tadpoles and tried to catch frogs.

She used to tell me her secrets. I still remember back when she leaned in real close and whispered in my right ear that she had walked in on her older sister changing in the bathroom. We used to giggle about how big her boobs were and wonder how many things she would bump into or knock over with them. We would pretend to be her, sticking out our chests, bumping into each other, or trees, or bushes, like, *oh, sorry, excuse me and my big boobs.* God... I would give anything to have tits like that now.

But, that next year, everything changed. That was the first time that dad forced me to touch his dick.

Honestly, it came out of nowhere, right out of left field. I mean, the day started out just like any other. Mom made us all breakfast, probably scrambled eggs and toast with extra strawberry jam, my favorite. Dad helped me get dressed while mom was struggling with toothless Tyler and baby Nikki. I remember throwing a fit about the sparkly pink shirt that he picked out. I wanted to wear my Pittsburg Steelers shirt, *again*, but he wouldn't let me. I cried into my Hannah Montana pillow for five minutes before I finally caved and stuck one arm through the sparkly pink shirt and walked around the house all pouty face and dramatic, like I was being tortured or something. Dad's raised voice finally made me put it on the right way and finish getting ready for school. That sad... disappointed... broken look in his eyes when I told him that I *hate him* was a look that I would see again later that evening.

It had rained the night before, and the ground was still wet, so when dad got home about an hour after us and saw our muddy footprints streaked through the hall, he flipped. He was sort of a neat freak. He would always say, "You're only as clean as you keep your house." But what did I care? I was nine years old and always getting yelled at for my messes.

"Ally! Ally, come here! What the hell is this?" He was standing in the entrance with the door still opened, pointing at our footprints lined through the hall and up the stairs to our rooms. His black suit looked wrinkled, and there was mud splattered up his trousers all the way to his butt.

"Get down here **now**, and clean this up!" He demanded when I peeked around the corner from the top of the steps.

"That wasn't me, that was Tyler." I tried to pass the blame like big sisters do.

"I don't give a shit who it was, I told you to get down here and clean it up." He was in a particularly grumpy mood and scrubbing at his dress shoes with an old t-shirt rag by the time I reached the last step.

"Why do I gotta do it?" I was testing his patience, and I knew it.

He met me at the bottom of the steps where I had stopped to protest.

"Because I said! You don't need any other God damned reason than that!" His voice was a kind of mean that I hadn't heard before.

Mom's concerned face rounded the hallway corner with Nikki on her hip.

"Daddy, shhh." Nikki put her tiny painted fingernail up to her lips like Mom always would.

Dad shot her a scolding look. "Don't you shush me!" It came out way crueler than what was called for.

"Now, Jim," Mom's eyebrows were scrunched, "settle down, settle down… it's only dirt, it'll clean up."

Dad searched for a clean spot on his rag to get the last bit of mud from the top of his right dress shoe.

"Don't you start, too. It's been a helluva day! You couldn't possibly imagine the carnage that we dug out of Will's Creek today! The bodies of these high school kids… mangled, twisted, naked, for God's sake, they had rope burns around their necks!"

"Jim!" Mom's eyes darted back and forth from me to Dad as if I had never watched TV before.

Dad gathered himself, "Look, I just want it cleaned up, and I want to sit down and relax. Is that too much to ask for? Is it?" He placed his shoes neatly together and tossed the dirty rag on a small muddy footprint.

"Go ahead, get it started." He was staring at me, and I could feel the tears start to build.

"Daaad, pleeease…I didn't do iiit." I begged.

"I've had about enough of this," he said to Mom as he loosened his tie and then his belt, wrapping it once around his hand, grasping the buckle.

"Jim! Jim!" The echo of Mom's voice rang out as he started in my direction.

My eyes practically popped out of my head as he marched his heavy feet toward me like he was on some sort of mission, or something. He grabbed me up, knelt down right in front of the steps, pulled my pants down, and lit my ass on fire. That was the first time he ever spanked me.

• • • • • • •

I could hear Mom and Dad still arguing while I sobbed on my bed. Puffy-eyed and snotty, and exhausted from raging out on my sheets and pillows, that were now mostly on the floor, I listened to their raised voices fighting back and forth. It lasted for a tense twenty minutes until I heard the stomping up the steps, the slam of their bedroom door, and the *clink* of ice cubes in a whiskey glass.

I must have fallen asleep, because my room was an eerie shade of black, except for the moonlight pushing through the window. Something woke me up. Some noise, perhaps. Or maybe just the feeling of being watched. Whatever it was, I wish it hadn't.

I laid there tangled in what was left of my sheets, listening. Through the distant outside hum of the freeway and the murmur of the downstairs TV, I thought I could hear breathing. Deep, shaky, drawn-out breathing. The type of breathing Mom would make while she was going through her school loan finances after chasing her dream to become a writer, one she mostly gave up when she discovered the *percs*. It was the same kind of breathing that Ms. Spurlock would do while she was grading our fourth-grade spelling tests. But this wasn't Mom's breathing... and it wasn't Ms. Spurlock's breathing. No. No, it was Dad's foul air.

Did he come up to apologize for hurting me? I wondered. *Is he going to tell me that he loves me and will never hurt me again? Or is he here to beat me some more?* I could hear the ice against his glass as he raised it up to his lips and slurped a large gulp. My eyes started to adjust and make out the tall, dark form leaning against the door frame. I peered through the darkness, trying to understand if what I was seeing was real. The wind blew in from the cracked-open window and pulled the curtains back to let the moonlight reveal his face. There was a deadness in his eyes. Evil, demon, dark, deadness. The burning of his stare made me squeeze my eyes shut and wish him away.

But he didn't leave. Instead, he walked closer, and closer, setting his glass on my nightstand after slurping the last of his whiskey. I could smell it on his breath. It was a heavy sour, a stale scent of bad decisions, wreaking of lies and delusions. I kept my eyes squeezed shut, hoping that when I opened them, it would be morning. I squeezed tightly and grimaced, trying to escape through my mind. I counted slowly to ten. *One. Two. Three. Four.* The breathing was at my ear. *Five. Six.* I could feel his wind hot on my cheek. *Seven. Eight. Nine...*

His large, bourboned hand slid across my mouth. He squeezed with more strength than I have ever felt in his touch. My eyes shot open with panic. His midnight eyes were staring right back at mine. I tried to scream. But he pressed harder, turning my lips numb and tingly. My breath was forced through my nose and loud against his hand.

"Don't. Make. A sound." He growled, unbuckling his belt with one hand.

He let his trousers fall to the floor. Their soft thud etching its way into my memory, just like the shake of his foot and rattle of his belt as he kicked his pants aside. They carved their sound waves onto the nerve endings of my darkest fears, my most painful horrors. His nails scratched the small of my back, leaving a hot, red trail as he ripped down my pants. Then, my bed springs groaned and creaked as his weight pressed and smothered me.

I tried to scream. I tried to make some kind of noise, *any kind of noise.* But my throat was dry, and my voice was lost in the confusion and horror of trying to understand what my father was getting ready to do to me. Instead, I forced my eyes shut, focusing on the black, on those little blotches of light, those small spots floating behind my eyelids, careless, unaware of what monster was just on the other side as I grabbed fists-full of sheets... and choked the softness right out of them.

• • • • • • •

Pain. Lots of pain. That's what I remember when I told Jessica about what had happened, and she didn't believe me. Gut wrenching pain and disappointment when she stopped coming over. Confusion. Anger. Hatred... *guilt.* Guilty. I felt guilty for ruining our friendship. I felt dirty, unwanted, like a broken barbie left outside, missing a limb and all of her clothes. I felt wrong. I felt like *I* did something wrong. Like, if I would have just been a better daughter... if I would have just *listened* and did what I was told. If I would have just been... better, then none of this would have happened. *None of this* would have happened.

Then, fear. I felt absolute terror the day I stayed after class to try and talk to Ms. Spurlock.

"Can I help you?" She looked up after all the children had gathered their notebooks and bookbags, and exited her room in an excited rumble of *what are you doing tonights* and *do you want to come overs*.

"Yes, ma'am. Can I... can I ask you something?"

She tossed her red grading pen, adjusted her thick glasses, and let out a lengthy annoyed huff.

"Sure. But make it quick. You don't want to miss the bus."

I shifted closer to her desk, awkward and shy. I had no idea what to say. I was clueless about how to talk about... rape.

"Well... you know my dad, right?" I started, blindly.

"Jim? Yeah, who *doesn't* know the famous Jim Handler? The detective that solved the Will's Creek Massacre case? Your father is a bit of a hero around here."

"Yeaaah... well, what if... what would happen... I mean..."

"Come on, out with it. We don't have all day." She pushed, tapping her papers into a neat stack on her desk.

With my hands cradling my books and looking at the pieces of an eraser on the floor beside Billy's desk, I searched for the right words to say.

"What if he... hurt someone?" I wasn't sure if that was what I wanted to say or not. But that's what came out when I spoke.

"What do you mean, *hurt someone?* Like, a criminal? Well, just between you and me, I hope he hurts them all." She was already annoyed and back shifting through her stack of quizzes.

"No. No, that's not what I mean. What if... what if he hurt... me?"

She stopped what she was doing and looked me up and down.

"You don't look hurt."

"Well, I am."

She removed her glasses, leaned back in her swivel chair, and stuck one end just between her lips.

"What are you trying to say, Ally? Just come out and say it, you're going to miss the bus."

"Dad... Dad... he..."

She was so obviously annoyed with my inability to shout out that my father has been raping me a few times a week. I mean, how are you even supposed to get help? How do you start a conversation like *that*? What are you supposed to say? *Hey, good afternoon. I thought that quiz was extra easy today. Oh, by the way, my dad puts his dick in my vagina.* You know... it's hard enough to talk to yourself about it. To come to terms with it. To try to rationalize it. To understand it. To convince your mind to *not* go insane from that kind of abuse... well, that's torture enough. I just didn't know how to talk to someone about it. I felt ashamed. I felt dirty. I felt wrong.

Then she let me have it. A gut punch on a full stomach. I nearly hurled.

"He's a hero, Ally. He's a smart man and a major contributor to not only this school but to the community, too. You should be proud of him. He's got so much on his mind with the type of important work that he does. You'd be best if you were just a good little girl and tried not to cause him any problems. He was there when my husband died, you know. I don't like to talk about it, especially with students. But, he spent all night there at the hospital after my husband's wreck. He was there beside us when he finally let go and passed on. It takes a special kind of man with a special kind of heart to do something like that."

Ms. Spurlock's patience was running thin. She dabbed at the corners of her eyes, swallowing down the tears and then cleared her throat.

Ally," she said softly, "is this about Jessica? I've noticed you two haven't been talking as much, lately. You know, these sorts of things happen with friends. Sometimes, you just outgrow each other. But you'll find other friends. You're a beautiful young girl. I mean look at those freckles! You won't have any trouble finding other friends."

My body was shaking with anger, with fear and frustration. She wouldn't even listen to me. She had no idea that her *hero* had been molesting his own daughter for months. I couldn't stand to look at her stupid face any longer.

"Thanks." I forced and hurried for the bus.

• • • • • •

Yeah, it really ate at me for a long time. It was... *hard*. Like, I just didn't understand why he was doing that to me and why nobody would listen. I still don't. But whatever. Eventually, I just got over it. I just... let it sink to the bottom of me. Besides, I had other things to worry about anyway, like school, art, and well... boys. I mean, he moved on to Nikki, and honestly, I missed his attention. I missed having my dad pay attention to me. You know, spend time with me... *love* me.

But, anyway, middle school was hell. Jim would take his frustrations out on me in the middle of the night, and I would take my frustrations out on everyone else. I'd take them out on *me*. I mean, look at my arms... look. This is what happens when you blame yourself. *This* is what I did to myself. And that's how I remember my early teens. There's really not much more to say about it. I was sexually abused by my father, and that's just something that I learned to live with.

Things are "better" now. I have a boyfriend, Brian, who I'm pretty sure only started liking me because he heard that I put out. It was a nasty rumor from the popular bitches that would get off on causing people like me pain. But if we're being honest, it's a rumor that's truer than I'd like for it to be. But, hey... it is what it is, right? Either way, I led Brian around on a leash for a few weeks, acting unimpressed with his flowers, notes and Little Debbie snacks at lunch, before I let him stick his hands down my pants. After all, a girl's got power in the pop of her curves. Truth is, I actually really like him. I think that's healthy, right? I mean, I might even... *love him.* He's basically all I have, to be honest. He... he just accepts me for who I am. He likes me because I *am* me.

I figured it was Jessica and her *skank club* that probably told him about the marks on my arms when we first started dating. Those bitches were always jealous that the star running back on our football team was more into someone like *me* than their peacock faces and push-up bras.

The day I showed him those scars, was the day that I started falling for him.

"What's that?" Brian asked when he first saw them.

I was embarrassed and tried to cover them up, even though I *wanted* him to see them, I *wanted* him to know my sickness. Instead, I just turned away and tugged at my sleeve.

"Nothing. It's nothing. Just... never mind."

He put his arms around me from behind and kissed my shoulder. He always knew how to love me, even from the beginning, and even though I had no idea how to love him back.

"Babe, I'm sorry. I had no idea... I..." He just held me and kissed me. He didn't need to say anything. I didn't need to say anything... but I wanted to tell him *everything*.

Eventually, I would. I would tell him every little detail, and he would rage out, even threaten to kill my father. Hearing the passion in his voice, the rage, the emotions firing off like the Fourth of July in his eyes, it made me believe him. I should've told him no. I should have saved him from the black eyes and broken nose that Dad served him when he tried to "man up." But the truth is, I kind of wanted him to win. Poor Brian and his big *stupid* heart, he still tries to convince me that "your scars are like your freckles, they just make you special." Bullshit.

The first time I tried cutting myself, all I left was just a scratch. I should have been in my seventh-grade science class, but overhearing Jessica's new best friend *Becca* making jokes about my black eye shadow and nails, made me want to escape, escape from... everything. I wanted to escape from school, from Byesville, from Ohio, from *here*... from this body, from that little girl cuffed to a bed and caged inside of my head... I used a purple mechanical pencil to dig into my forearm in the last bathroom stall, right beside the "call Ally for a good time" graffiti and just a few feet away from the guidance counselor's office.

Hmm. Brian... poor, hopeless, romantic, Brian. He thinks that I should just run away with him. Like that's going to solve everything. You know, I pity him with all of his feelings and emotions. He thinks we should steal my dad's wallet, truck, and gun. You know, do a real Bonnie and Clyde thing. Run off together, just me and him... robbing banks, or gas stations... maybe even head down to Florida... or maybe California. A place where no one will know us. A place where we can be anybody we want to be, where we can do anything we want to do. Somewhere warm and sunny. Somewhere happy.

He thinks we should run away. Maybe we will.

I wonder what these scars will look like with a nice, golden tan.

FOUR.
TYLER

2017, December

I love this stupid chair.

Alright, well, you know, football's pretty much my life. I switched to receiver this year. Did you happen to see my winning touchdown catch against Cambridge? Oh, man... it was glorious. You should have seen the girls lining up to get my number. I was like a rockstar, getting more ass than a toilet seat. You know what I mean? Wait, sorry, can I say that here? You said not to hold back. That this was a place to express myself. You told me to say whatever comes to mind, as long as it's honest and on topic. Right?

Alright. Well, anyway, Coach thinks there'll be scouts in the stands next year. Maybe a scholarship or two will be thrown my way. I guess all that extra time in the weight room is paying off. I even have a path cut into the hill at my house from doing hill sprints in my eighth-grade championship cleats. They're a little worn out now, though. There's a hole starting to break through, just underneath the Under Armour symbol on the right one. That won't stop me though. I forget what football movie it was, but after I saw them run the hill, I figured, what the heck... I'll give it a try. I used dad's weed eater to clear the tall grass last summer, and it wasn't long before I had a dirt path worn up and down it. Did I mention that I can do 58 pushups in a row? That's the third highest on the team. Chase can only do 43. You can definitely tell a difference between his pecs and mine in the shower.

Damn. The shower. Ours doesn't even have a door anymore. Well, I mean... there's a curtain on the shower, but dad removed the bathroom door and nailed up a sheet, instead. He made us all stand there and watch as he removed the door from the hinges, pulled a sheet from the linen closet in the hallway, flung it open furiously, and hammered three nails into it. Mom said that we needed our privacy, but he insisted that it was a safety issue. He didn't trust us around the cleaning supplies after Ally ended up in the hospital.

I'd catch him outside the door every now and then, leaning against the door frame to his room, pretending to read one of his cop magazines, his faint shadow through the sheet turning the page, lifting his head often. I knew what he was doing, he did it to all of us. I mean, it's not *that* big of a deal. Yeah, he sees us naked, so what? He used to change our diapers. Besides, Ally's been walking around the house topless. *Yeah, sure, you forgot to bring your clothes into the bathroom, again.* I just think she's mental and a real attention seeker. She's been over the top ever since... well... ever since Dad has been more focused on Nikki.

She's kind of a bitch, actually. She always has this poor attitude. Like, the other day, when all of a sudden, she made such a big deal out of me running into the bathroom to grab my deodorant while she was in the shower. Like, who cares? Yeah... okay, *sometimes* I watch her shower. But what's the big deal? Dad does it. She doesn't throw a fit over that! Then she had to go and tell him all about it like I was some sort of criminal or something.

Dad was like, "What are you doing? Stop watching your sister shower." He said it just like he would when talking to Special Agent Gibbs on TV after two or three trips to the whiskey cabinet.

I laughed it off. "They're just boobs, Dad. Well, *sort of.*" I turned and laughed at her. "It's not a big deal."

She growled and crossed her arms over her chest. "You're such an asshole! Just leave me alone!" Then, she stomped upstairs to pout in her room.

Dad raised his wet whiskey glass and took a deep drag. His eyes never left the TV as his arm casually fell back into his lap. I waited there a second or two, thinking he might say something else. But he didn't. He just clicked the volume up twice and set the remote on the coffee table.

I smiled the whole way back, upstairs to my room.

• • • • •

Well, I've been having this dream ever since Nikki spoke up. I'm four or five years old, I think. Everyone is over for Ally's birthday party. Some of her school friends are there, Jessica brings this big gift, it's an artist set. I never see Ally open it, but I can see her playing with it. She's drawing a picture of her and Jessica on the rope swing at Jessica's house. It's one of those typical childhood pictures, you know? It's got that big yellow sun in the upper right-hand corner with the squiggly lines coming out of it. There's a tall bushy tree in the middle with different colors of green for the leaves, and dark, heavy lines of brown for the trunk. It even has a squirrel hole in the trunk of it. I can see the red, purple, and yellow flowers in the little strokes of grass. There are two fishing poles, I mean, I *think* they're fishing poles. They kind of look like sticks with an oversized letter J dangling from a short string. I see the poles are on the ground to the left of the tree. The swing is on the right-hand side, coming down from the one horizontal branch jetting out across the page. There is a stick figure with long blonde hair sitting on the swing, and a stick figure with a dark ponytail pushing her from behind. They are wearing matching jeans and red shirts. I watch her draw a large bubble coming from each stick figure's head. In the one coming from the blonde, it says, "Ha, Ha," inside. Then, in the one coming from the dark-haired girl, it reads "Best Friends 4-ever."

Some of Dad's cop friends are there. It's loud. Everyone is talking and laughing. Everyone is happy and getting along. Mom and Dad are side by side with one arm wrapped around each other's waist. They're talking to some of Dad's police buddies. It must be something funny because they're all cracking up.

Then, I'm in the kitchen, watching Dad pour a full glass from a half-empty Jim Beam bottle. He turns around to see me.

"Hey, sport. Whatcha got there?" He bends down to my level.

I slowly reach out my little hand. All I can see is my blurry arm stretching out in front of me. I'm squeezing something in my tiny fist. It starts to come into focus. I can feel how badly I want Dad to see whatever I have in my hand. I stretch my arm all the way out, as close to his face as I can reach. Then, it comes into focus, and I can see what I'm holding.

Clenched in my fist is my blood-soaked, Batman underwear.

"Well, that's alright, buddy. No one can see." He said as if I had just whispered a secret and he was confirming that it was safe with him.

Next thing I know, I'm in the basement closet. It's dark, but I know that there are two people in the closet with me. I feel their presence. I feel their eyes feasting on me. I feel naked. I feel completely and totally exposed.

I can hear their deep voices, but I can only understand a couple of words.

"Mouth shut."

"I'll watch."

"Never tell."

"Safe."

"Quiet."

"Hurry."

There is a sharp pain at my rear. I can feel my body jerking back and forth. It's in slow motion now. My hands are against the cold, dark wall. There are groans and grunts that sound like thunder.

"Almost done."

"Me too."

My body jerks faster and faster. More thunder. Lightening. Pain. And an un-Godly ROAR.

Next thing I know. I'm at the kid's table in the living room eating cake and ice cream. Everyone is laughing around me, but I'm not. Everyone is happy, but me.

I look up from my bowl of Neapolitan ice cream and chocolate cake to see Dad staring at me from the kitchen door.

He winks. And slides his thumb across his throat.

Then, I wake up gasping for air, sweaty, trapped by the sheets at my ankles, sideways on my bed, my hands pressing against the wall. I want to scream, but my mouth won't open. I can barely force a growl into my throat.

I've been having this dream a lot, lately. It's one of those dreams that feel so real. I mean, I can feel *everything*... the vibrations of music playing in the corner, the heat of friends and family filling the dampness of our house, eyes watching me... a stabbing pain behind me.

Sometimes, I believe it. Sometimes... I think it *is* real.

•   •   •

The incident? I mean, I wouldn't call it an *incident*. You know, just boys horsing around. Boys will be boys, right? Ha. Ha. Look, it's really not that big of a deal. I don't know why everyone is so bent out of shape about it. *Nooo*, I'm playing with my hair because... because I need something to do with my hands. For real, he didn't even get hurt. He was just scared. Who doesn't like a good prank every now and then? Right? C'mon. I mean, you should've seen his face... it was glorious.

Well, it happened this summer during two-a-days conditioning for football. This year sucked even more than my freshman year. I think it was hotter. Or maybe coach just ran us more. Either way, I wasn't the only one to throw up. Ha. Ha. There was a line of us, all hunched over on the sideline, I don't know how many, maybe five or six of us. We were in our new matching white shorts (complete with dirty sweat stains) and orange t-shirts that the booster's rotisserie chicken sale bought for us this year. Honestly, I thought we looked gay. *Sorry, I mean silly.* We looked silly, like a bunch of douchebags out there running around in matching dresses, or something. Hell, we were more color-coordinated than the cheerleaders. Ha. Ha. The only way to tell us apart were the names taped to the front of our helmets... so Coach knew who to yell at.

It had to be 100 degrees on the practice field. I can remember pointing out the heat waves to Robbie, our jacked, *I mean the dude's ripped*, starting running back, and then, making some stupid joke about the desert and war. We call it, The Oven. August in Ohio is Hell. Even during warmups, our jumping jacks stirred up this cloud of dust that would make your teeth gritty. We'd have brown streaks of sweat rolling down our faces. We called it *war paint*. Coach called it... Colt Blood. He's a bit of "pride" freak. For those two weeks, every huddle break, he'd have us all yell "Ahh... 1, 2, 3, colt pride!" It went well with our matching *dresses*. Ha. Ha.

But anyway, it was hot. We were dirty. We were exhausted. We were chewed up and spit out. And we were doing fourth-quarter drills... which is, running gassers and then trying to run a play. But Chase kept *fffuuu*... uh, I mean, "messing up." C'mon, he's the quarterback, just a sophomore, but still, he should know how to run a simple triple-option. Right? Well, he didn't. His footwork was all jacked up. He kept tripping over Robbie, our running back. Looking like a fool. Making us *all* look like fools.

You should've seen coach raising Hell. I mean, if we didn't have to run so many gassers, I would've laughed about it all.

Honestly, though... I think he was still a little hungover from Jay's party. So was I, well before I sweat it all out. I told him... I said, "Chase, dude, seriously... get your shit together. We're gonna be here all day."

"Damn it, I know. I got this."

He always says *I got this,* even when he clearly doesn't.

Well, he finally did get it. We even ran the same play five times in a row without messing it up.

Then, Coach said that it'd come down to one final play... if we got it right, we'd be done for the day. But, if we got it wrong, more gassers.

It was a simple play. A pass play. I wish Coach would've called my number. But he didn't. He called on some freshman receiver. I don't even know his name, yet. Some scrawny, lanky kid. He looked like he could be a high jumper during track season. We just called him Green Bean.

He nearly *shit-a-brick* when Coach called him out on the field.

"Alright, gents... Green Bean, here, is going to be our number one on this play. If he catches it, we go home. If not, we run more gassers. Got it? Good."

Green Bean shook his facemask up and down, slowly, like he wasn't really sure what Coach had just said.

"Ok, gents... let's show Green Bean a little support. This could be any one of us, called upon in any game, to pull our weight, to have your back. And when it comes down to having your number called, you can bet your ass that you will look to your left and right, to the guy next to ya... you'll look right into his shit-brown eyes... and you'll know... you'll know that he's got your six, that he has your back, that he's right there in the trenches with you. You'll know that you can count on him, just like he can count on you. That's a team, gents. That's what we're here to learn... how to trust each other."

Coach looked around and peered into each and every one of our souls, kneeling in that semi-circle of sweat, stink, and smeared blood.

"Alright, Green Bean. You're up. *I-right, 22 option, crisscross deep.* Run it."

All Green Bean had to do was catch a long crossing pattern in the middle of the field. Cake. A *freakin'* piece of cake.

Green Bean lined up on the left. I could see his leg muscles twitching. He nearly tripped over his own awkward feet at the snap of the ball. He took off, the dust following. All he had to do was go up the field fifteen yards, then cross behind the shallow crosser coming in from the right. Like I said, simple. But no. Green Bean ran straight down the field twenty yards and stopped. He had no idea what to do.

Coach blew his whistle in a series of shrieks.

"What the *flippin' hell* was that, Green Bean!?" Coach yelled from behind the offense.

Green Bean came running back with his hands out.

"I thought I had the seam route?"

"Greeeen Beaaan... nooo." Coach said. "You're the number one on this play! You're the *cross*. You do the crossing route!"

Green Bean let out a long heavy breath from low shoulders. He kicked at the dirt and hit his helmet.

"Don't give up. Run it again!" Coach blew his whistle.

We cheered him on, tried to give him a little pick-me-up, you know?

So, he ran it, again, and this time, he ran the *right* route. Haha. The ball was nearly perfect. A high arcing spiral, just a hair in front of him. Green Bean reached out for it. It hit his hands in stride. He juggled it once, and then it hit the ground, bounced, and spun out of bounds. He *freakin'* dropped it. I mean, a perfect pass. And he dropped it.

Man, I wish Coach would've called my number.

Well, we ran until we puked. I think Coach wanted to teach us something. But I didn't care what it was at that point. I just knew that Green Bean was going to get *his*. He had it coming.

When we got back up to the locker-room, the coaches had a meeting in the Coach's Office while we hit the showers.

The *incident* all started with one of the linemen, a big guy we call Chunk. He's a junior, not too bright, but he could push through a defensive lineman like he was a swinging door. He was unwrapping the tape from his wrists, soaked, and still breathing heavy.

"I think I might have green beans for dinner tonight. What do you think about that, Green Bean?"

Green Bean was sitting on the bench across from him with his head down, staring at his hands.

"Ok." He said.

But that wasn't the answer that Chunk was looking for.

"Well, maybe I should just take a bite out of you first." Chunk was on his feet. Sort of awkward, funny even, in just his gray, sweat-soaked, boxer-briefs.

Green Bean looked up to read Chunks face. He looked dead serious, and the locker-room died down to a low murmur.

"Look, man, I'm sorry. I'm *really* sorry. I don't know what happened. I don't know how I dropped it." He shook his head and bit his lower lip. "But, it won't happen again."

"You're damn right it won't. Not if you want to be on *this* team."

"I do, man. I love football. I promise. I promise I won't suck anymore."

Chunk grabbed the front of his boxers.

"Maybe you should suck on this."

He started walking from his side of the locker room toward Green Bean. Green Bean stood up, not knowing what to do.

"Grab him." Chunk said to his linemen buddies laughing beside him.

Three of the linemen grabbed hold of Green Bean, picked him up off of his feet, and forced him down on the nasty locker-room floor.

Chunk hovered over his face.

"How bad do you want to be on this team?"

Green Bean, not knowing whether to laugh or cry, gave up and stopped squirming.

"Real bad. I swear."

"Bad enough to suck on *deez nuts*"? Chunk squatted above his face so that his sweaty underwear were just inches above Green Beans nose.

"Go on, open up, you freshman turd."

The locker room was circled around them, smiling, laughing, egging the whole thing on.

"Do it." Someone shouted.

"Come on, Green Bean. Show him how much you love football," another one screamed.

Chunk lingered above his nose for a few seconds and then stood up laughing.

"Damn, Green Bean, I think you were *really* gonna do it."

Everyone started laughing.

"Alright. Alright. Let him go. Let him up. I'm just playing around." Chunk reached out to help him up.

"Wait!" I shouted. "Wait a second! That's it? That's all? He made us run 'til we puked!"

All eyes were on me now. I could feel their stares. I didn't like it. But, I was just getting started.

Green Bean started to get up.

"No. No, buddy. You don't get off that easily. Hold him down." I said, quickly undressing.

A few guys started laughing. Others looked concerned. But two linemen grabbed him again and held him still.

"Hold him! Hold him still," I said as I stood over him in my white boxer-briefs.

The linemen pinning him there were laughing. Green Bean had an uncomfortable smirk on his face. He had no idea if I was kidding or being totally serious.

I was being totally serious.

I squatted over his face, just like Chunk had done. My dirty, raunchy boxers were right in his eyes. The boys were all laughing. They thought it was hilarious. You know, just some freshman hazing, some prank that's pretty common between boys. It wasn't that big of a deal.

But then, his juggling of the football flashed into my head. I could feel the rage rising. I saw the ball spinning on the ground, rolling out of bounds. My teeth started to shake from clenching my jaw. I could taste the dust, the sweat, and the puke, from running so many gassers. I felt the drop in my stomach, like just before I threw up along the sidelines.

I don't know what made me do it. Maybe the anger. Maybe the rage. Or maybe that it just didn't feel *wrong*.

I pulled down my boxers and slapped my dick on his forehead.

"Dude! C'mon! Get off of him!" Chase pushed me away from him. "What the hell is wrong with you?!"

I pulled up my boxers and looked around at the frozen faces staring back at me. A few kids were smiling, maybe even laughing. Some looked disgusted, some in shock.

Green Bean was frantically rubbing at his forehead. He got to his feet quickly, still rubbing. "You're an asshole!" He fired.

Then, he sat down in front of his locker, defeated, and started to cry.

Standing there naked, I felt my lips stretching into an evil smile.

"Hey. Guys. C'mon. It's not that big of a deal."

FIVE.
ASHLEY

2018, January

Yeah, no, I'm fine… I'm just… exhausted.

You know, things weren't always like this. I wasn't always this dejected. Life wasn't always this catastrophic. My husband… *Jim*… hasn't always been this… this… *plague.* I didn't willingly marry Lucifer. He transformed. He changed. His light faded. He was sucked into the darkness of his past. Do you know what I mean?

No, I'm not trying to defend him, or his actions. What he's done to this family is *damning,* to say the least. I just need you to know that there used to be a *real* person in there. Jim used to… he used to **love**. He used to love *me*. He used to laugh and care and feel. He used to want to save the world. He had a hunger to cleanse this town of all of its filth; to put evil behind bars, or under the ground. That's what attracted me to him. That's why I married him. Because he promised to be my hero! He saved me from my adolescent martyrdom, he pulled me out of that hole. He took me away from the hell that I lived in, from the stepfather that took whatever he wanted from me whenever he wanted it. He… he saved me. And now… well…

Look, we all have demons. You can't deny me that. But sometimes, the things that we bury vibrate their way back to the top, like rocks in a bucket of sand. The more we shake up our existence, the more these stones break the surface.

Having Tyler shook Jim's world. All of a sudden, all of these repressed memories came dancing to the surface. Just like that, Jim saw his *own childhood abuse* when he looked at our child. He saw his *own father* doing the same things to him that Jim would later do to his own children. How strange, how sickening, how… *linear* the cycle of abuse.

It's a damn web. A trap. It's this ill plot in a psychological thriller. I was mentally and physically assaulted by my stepfather. Jim saved me. He took me away from there, and gave me hope, life, and love... only to become exactly what I needed to be rescued from in the first place. Jim, who came from the Devil's den himself, confessed it all to me one drunken evening. He confessed to me how he was sexually tortured by his father *and* his father's greedy friends, only to turn around and put his own children through that same gauntlet.

It is a damn plague! A level **six** epidemic! It's a path to world destruction, this chain linked gene of mental illness, these psychotic episodes of sexual rage; they're a pile of shattered glass that we all just sweep under the rug, left there to rip into our skin another day.

How can this be?! How can we say that we are loving creatures, that we are humane, charitable, and intelligent beings... if we can't recognize, admit, or even **talk** about these appalling travesties to humanity, let alone, solve them? *We* are our own abusers.

I used to burn myself with cigarettes when I was seventeen.

I thought feeling the pain would let me know that I was still alive. I thought that hurting myself would... would... *teach me* some sort of lesson. Like, if I could just slap myself right out of it, then I would wake up and start living for myself. Does that make any sense? Is that therapeutic? Hurting yourself to make yourself want to live? It sounds disgusting, doesn't it? The desperation that it takes to blame yourself for something that someone else has done to you... it *is* disgusting. I think what I hated the most about me, was my lack of courage. I knew that I needed to do something, *anything*... to stop my stepfather from hurting me. But I *allowed* it to go on. Hell, for a while I even thought that I *deserved* it.

Until Jim came along. Then, I knew that life could be sweet. He used to pick flowers for me along the road on our way home from school. The white and yellow ones that grow wild in the spring. He would pull a small vine from the brush and tie it in a bow around the stems. He said that I was as beautiful and as wild as those flowers. He told me that I **was** those flowers... and anytime that I felt like hurting myself, I should just pluck off a petal, crumble it up in my hand, feel the moisture, the stickiness, the soft pieces of destruction rolling between my fingers, and then open my hand to look at what a beautiful mess I had created... and to know that I am fully capable of being beautiful *even if I am* in pieces.

Jim put my stepfather in the hospital the day that we ran off to get married. I was two weeks green at eighteen, and Jim was just shy of twenty-two. He was working construction, saving up to study criminal justice, and I was a few days from graduating high school. He picked me up from school like he always did, and we drove out to Seneca Lake. I loved to sit on the tailgate of his old stepside Chevy, parked at one of the pull-off spots along the water's edge. I would hold onto his strong arm and rest my head onto his shoulder, watching the gleaming ripples break onto the sandy pieces of shale stone. Every now and then a couple of ducks would fly by, and I would joke about how that could be us someday, free and soring to wherever the wind would take us.

That sunny day, he leaned in to kiss me and said: "let's do it."

He hopped off the tailgate, ran into the trees beside us, came back out with a smile, and lifted me off the tailgate. He knelt to a knee, and in the trickling crash of dirty lake water and distant quacks of ducks flying away, he asked me to marry him. He didn't have a ring, of course, but he asked for me to stick out my hand, anyway. Then, he tied a vine into a bow around my ring finger. Of course, I said yes! He was my salvation! He was the feeling of life, he was the wind, the warm sun, the splash of water, the smell of dirt and earth... he was the world to me.

We ran home to get a few things before we rode off into the sunset, metaphorically and literally. That old Chevy slid to a stop in my gravel driveway. That Garth Brooks' country hit, *Ain't Going Down 'Til The Sun Comes Up*, pounded at the speakers, and died at the twist of the key. We ran into the house holding hands.

That's when my stepfather stopped us.

"Where the hell have you been?"

"At the lake... *daddy*." He forced me to call him daddy ever since I was three.

"Well, lose your friend, it's time for you to make dinner."

"I'm not making dinner tonight. I'm leaving."

He shot us a look of confused anger from his living room armchair.

"Like hell you are! Now get your ass in the kitchen and make me something to eat."

Jim hated when he spoke to me like that.

"No, I don't think that's going to happen tonight," Jim said. "And maybe you should learn how to talk a little nicer to your stepdaughter."

"No one asked you for your two cents, boy. Now shut up, and get out of my house." He took a swig from his Old Milwaukee, rattled it around, and tossed the empty can towards a full trashcan. It skidded across the floor and crashed into one of the three other empty cans starting to make a pile.

Jim shook his head and smiled to comfort me.

"Run up and pack a bag, babe. I'll handle him."

I ran upstairs to pack a few things, and it wasn't long before I heard the rumble and felt the walls shake. By the time I hustled back down the steps, Jim was wiping blood from his lip, and my stepfather was lying unconscious in his own blood underneath a head-sized hole in the wall.

We drove most of the night until we bumped into this quiet little town. We got married at the Cambridge Courthouse that next day.

For what it's worth, we had several years of happiness, in the beginning, while we both got our degrees. Life was good back then. We took our time. We waited to have kids until we were sure that we were ready. Hold on, let's be honest, *are we really ever ready?* But, I'll never forget the look of love in his eyes the day that Ally was born.

It was a look that was *not duplicated* when the doctor finally placed Tyler into his cradled arms.

· · · · ·

It's hard to say this... I've never actually told anyone this before but given the circumstances, and the "honesty atmosphere," I guess it's safe to say...

Nikki... was a rape baby... by my **own husband**.

Hell, I should've seen the signs. I should have been more vigilant, more perceptive. But you know, it's a funny thing, what we do with our minds, convincing ourselves that what we see isn't *actually* there. I mean, how could a man that was so loving, sooo... *heroic*, my Hercules... or Cronus, rather... how could a man like that, a father, do something so evil?

He was never the same man after Tyler was born. It was like a switch flipped inside his psyche, and all of a sudden, he was the *real* American Psycho. It came in spurts, in waves. Small, gradual white caps, rolling in on our perfect little beach. He let his mind go, gradually at first, like a melting popsicle in the August sun. When I finally realized that I was standing there holding onto nothing but the stick, it was too late. My hands were just as messy as his, sticky, and red. Regrettably, I spent too many years in denial.

I just kept making excuses for him. *Oh, it must've been another hard day at work. He's just stressed out. He still loves us, but he has a lot on his mind. I couldn't possibly understand what he goes through each day.* Yes, I tried to rationalize his actions. And when that didn't work, I tried to justify them. *Well, Ashley, if you would've just cleaned up the house before he got home. Maybe if you weren't high all the time. He needs to let it out, or he'll explode.*

The night that he forced himself inside of me... that should've been the night that I left him.

He got home late, again. He'd been out at the bar with a few of the other cops on his shift. I could smell it on him, stale fermented air, cigars, fried food, and rage. It rushed in like a tidal wave through the door and lingered on the rug where he stood, stumbling while he tried to undress.

"Dinner's in the oven," I said wrapping the dragging blanket tighter around my shoulders as I made my way back upstairs to bed. I decided to just let him in, myself, after listening to his key poke at the keyhole and rattle on the porch for five minutes while Shooter barked and growled in the yard. I wanted no part of *this* Jim. The drunk rage monster that fires on whiskey fuel and snide remarks.

He had started to stay out drinking more frequently after his promotion to Sergeant. At the time, I thought the added weight of responsibility was more taxing than he could handle. But now I realize that he was at war with a more *personal* demon than just work.

His voice was heavy and smoky. "I ate."

"Okay," I muttered halfway up the steps.

I was close to the top when I heard him stumble and ask for help. I should have never hesitated. I should've never turned around. Then maybe that night would have been different. But... then again, maybe Nikki would never have been born.

"Help me." He said from his back, reaching for the one untied shoe still on his foot.

I should've just gone to bed and been done with it. But, seeing him so helpless, so weak, so *little*... I felt empowered to have some sort of control over him. So, I sluggishly made my way back down the stairs to help him remove his shoe and pants.

He grabbed my butt as I held him up.

"Not now, Jim. It's time for bed."

He squeezed my cheeks and moaned.

"Come on. Up the steps. Bedtime." I slapped his hand away, talking to him like I would talk to Ally at bedtime. I nearly had to drag him toward the stairs.

"No!"

He shifted his weight from my shoulders to his feet, leaned back and smacked me across the face.

Just like that, the switch had flipped.

I turned by the force of his hand and covered my face.

"Jim! No! Stop! Please!"

He half tackled, half fell onto me right there in the hallway at the bottom of the steps. Before I knew what to do, he was on top of me, slobbering all over my face and neck. A *real turn-on* for a half-asleep, angry woman.

"Jim. Jim! Quit! Stop it!" I tried to push him off me, but he was dead weight.

He sat up, pinning my waist under his, and forced my arms to the floor.

"Stop moving." He was looking at me but wasn't there. He was somewhere else, buried deep in a drunken state of painful, adolescent emotions that were never mended.

He ripped and ravaged my blanket and t-shirt, smacking away my protests until there were no more. Then, in a twisting fistful, he yanked off my panties.

"Jim..." I uttered one last plea before he had his way with me.

$$\bullet \quad \bullet \quad \bullet \quad \bullet \quad \bullet \quad \bullet$$

After that night, I tried to drown myself in alcohol until I realized that I was pregnant.

Since it was his idea not to have any more after Tyler, he wasn't excited when he came home from work and found me crying in the bathroom holding a positive pregnancy test. There was no joy, it wasn't a happy moment. Instead, he yelled at me as if it were my fault.

"How could you let this happen? We agreed, no more kids!" He slammed the test into the trashcan as if that would make the pregnancy disappear.

I shuddered at the sink, reaching for a bottle of painkillers, reliving exactly how it had happened. *Well, Jim, it happened from you raping me at the bottom of the stairs two months ago, asshole!* I don't know how many pills I popped, I just remember crying all night, wondering what had happened to our family.

After she was born, I suffered from postpartum depression. Jim still blamed me for the pregnancy, but at least he stopped hitting me for a little while. At first, I tried to drink it all away. And it worked for a short spell. I even felt proud that I had the control to handle it *myself.* I felt like a real Hemingway or Poe. Writing and drinking, drinking and writing. For a few short years, I *was* in control.

But, ultimately, the pain from his drunkest nights would never go away. After a rough "fall down the stairs," my doctor prescribed Percocet for the pain. Well, it wasn't long before I became addicted. They were so good at making me feel so numb. They were perfect for letting me escape. And I didn't care how it went away, I just needed the misery to stop. I slowly fell deep into a dark hole of prescription medication and alcohol. It was my sole salvation, my only escape... my further damnation.

I wasn't high every day. I was still a *good* mother. I went to all of Tyler's t-ball and biddy league games. I helped Ally with her dance and music recitals. I did... *stuff*... with Nikki. I was a good mom. I was a *good mom.*

Jim got more abusive as the years went by. Then, he would try to make up for it by buying us anything we wanted. Underneath all of that damage, I still believed that he loved me. And I think, somewhere... somewhere down inside of me, I still loved him, too.

Some days were even calm, sweet days. There were marvelous parties and formal balls with the police department, where I'd get to wear a dress and heels, and him looking so handsome in his suit. We would dance the night away, back then. I would flaunt the diamond earrings and flashy necklace he got me for our fifth anniversary. You know, I felt special *some* days. And I admired the school events for the children – when we were more of a family than we were at home. But even at home, *some* days were still decent, *some* days we were still a loving family.

That's about the time that Ally ran away *and* tried to kill herself.

There had grown a huge disconnect between my children and me. As they grew, they distanced themselves from me... or maybe me from them. Honestly, I don't know what happened. I don't know what made us stop being there for each other. It just seemed to unfold that way, like one of those memory foam toppers out of the package, we just gradually expanded our distance. I thought that maybe it was just the *teen* in them. But I didn't have a clue as to how gone they really were. Well, not until Ally drank the bathroom cleaning supplies, and I found her in her vomit on the bathroom floor. If it weren't for the three glasses of wine, I wouldn't have moved from the couch. She would have just laid there dying while I was comfortable and high on the downstairs sofa. I hate myself for that. I hate myself for losing my children.

The truth is, I dug myself in deeper and deeper until I couldn't see the light. And by then, I was so numb to the pain that this dysfunctional life just seemed normal. It *felt* normal. Like, *oh, it's just Jim hitting me, again. He'll stop eventually and leave me alone. Then, I'll get some new shoes or jewelry. No big deal.* This was the world that we were living in. Like some thriller crime novel where the main characters are doing something so illogical, so annoying, so painful and self-inflicting, that while you are frustratingly flipping through the pages reading, you are begging them to stop, pleading with them to find the courage to do what they need to do, yelling at them to just open their eyes.

I wish someone would have begged me to stop.

SIX.
JIM

2018, May

Let's just get one thing straight, here–I never did whatever it is that they say I did– and I don't need this. Matter of fact, if it wasn't court ordered, I'd completely blow it off, if we're "being honest."

My side of the story? What is there to tell? I have three spoiled little brats and a gold-digging wife who has no respect for the man of the house. Yes, the man of the house. Some families still believe in that tradition. I certainly do. I'm the breadwinner, I pay the bills, it's *my* land, it's *my* house... and I have authority over what happens in *my* house. End of story. If someone steps out of line and needs to be reprimanded, then, by all means, they will get reprimanded. It's that simple.

You know what's wrong with the world today? No discipline. That's right. All of these kids are running around with their faces stuck in their iPhones and iPads, having no clue as to what's going on around them, no respect for order, or tradition, or power.

Yes, power. It's what runs this country. It's what drives every decision, forces every move we make. Power. People will steal for it, fight for it, even kill for it. Believe me, I've seen it all in my line of work. People want power, whether they'll admit it or not. They *need* it! And, they will do whatever it takes to get it. Think about it, Doc, that's how we're raised, that's how we're trained in school, organized in our careers, manipulated by our government... it's all about *power*.

Let me tell you about **power**. By the time I was seven years old, my father had already taught me two important lessons about power. *Number one:* He has all the authority under his roof. *And number two:* If you want that to change, then do something about it.

You see, growing up, we lived a few miles outside of town, just off a narrow, pot-holed, and gravel road. It was the country as far as I was concerned. We ran through the sprinkler when it was hot, and we put wood on the fire when it was cold. My father worked construction; my mother kept the house clean and warm food on the table. We weren't poor, but we weren't rich either. We kept a few chickens, goats, and horses in the barn, I was in charge of tending to the goats and chickens, while my older brother tended to horses.

Even at the age of five, my father was trying to teach me something about life– about power. Each morning before school, and each evening after school, we would do our chores. We'd feed the animals and make *damn sure* that our rooms were clean. Trust me, it didn't take too many whips from my father's leather belt to understand how important it was to keep things tidy. He would often tell us, "I spend all day in the dirt for my family, and the last thing I want at the end of a long, hard day, is to come home to filth."

Anyway, there was this one goat, I remember quite well, that would give me all kinds of hell while I tried to do the feeding. He would charge from behind and ram me with his horns or, if I got too close, he would kick me to the mud. It's sort of funny now looking back on it, but I wasn't laughing back then. That goat tormented my life for the greater part of my kindergarten year. It became so traumatic that I was scared to go do my chores. So, some days I just wouldn't do them. Well, my father certainly didn't appreciate his children not doing what was demanded of them... and I would get the belt, but there were days where I'd rather have the belt than deal with that damned goat.

I was absolutely between a rock and a hard place. My father understood my predicament, but he didn't back off. I suppose he was doing his best to try and teach me something. Then, out of pure sympathy, frustration, *or embarrassment,* he gave me some advice. He said, "Son, you can either let that goat push you around, or you can walk into that pen with your chest out and head high, and let that goat know that **you're in charge**." What a bold concept for a five-year-old to understand– that the power either belonged to the goat... or to me.

I did just that. I walked out to that pen with my chest out and head high, and I told that goat in my best Hulk Hogan voice that he better leave me alone or I would whip him with the stick in my hand. We met head to head when I entered the pen. Without hesitating, he headbutted me right in the forehead before I could even close the gate – before I could even swing my stick. Well,

I fell backward into the mud, laid there, and cried. After a few minutes, I got up rubbing my head, slammed the gate shut and threw the bucket of food over the fence. It was a painful walk back to the house, bruised, bloodied, and defeated.

That didn't go over so well with Dad. He wasn't impressed with the guts it took to face my fears. I think he was more embarrassed than angry about my defeat. But, either way, he wasn't happy that I conceded my power to some damn goat. He let me feel his disappointment with five belt whips across my rear-end. With blood and tears rolling down my face, he beat it into me, that he wasn't about to raise some chicken-shit kid.

That's when he taught me a lesson that I'll never forget: *power isn't given, it's something that you **take**.*

He dragged me outside by the shirt collar to the pen. With dried blood and tears on my puffy red face, he swung open that fence and demanded that I take back the power that I gave up to that goat. I was **five years old**... trying to understand what the hell my dad was talking about. He stood there and watched as I balled my eyes out trying to muster the gall to *fight* this bully of a goat.

It was no use, I couldn't hack it. Eventually, he had to step in. There was no winning for me. That goat had kicked me, rammed me, trampled me, and ripped me open. I was a complete failure, and my father let me know it. He took out his pocketknife and placed it in my shaky little hand. He told me that it was time to man up, that it was time to take back my power, my *manhood*, or I would face a hundred lashes from the belt. Then, my father grabbed ahold of the goat's horns and twisted it down to the ground. There, he lifted it head up to the sky, exposing its trembling neck, and demanded that I *cut it open*.

I battled that decision for longer than I should have. The entire time, my father was yelling with that poor goat pinned in the mud, crying out gurgled calls for help, shaking, and anticipating its neck to be ripped open by my tiny hand.

"Do it!" He yelled, covered in mud.

"I can't! I can't do it!" I cried.

"There is no can't, boy, now do what I tell ya!" He pulled its head higher toward the fading sky as if that would make it easier for me to go through with it.

I took a couple of steps toward them, my knees nearly giving out with each slurp of muck grabbing at my boots. I shifted the knife in my hand, felt its cold steel, its weight, its power. I squeezed it tightly, ready to commit. I was inches away from its neck. I could see its veins pumping blood up rapidly to wide eyes and muffled terrified cries. I extended the sharp, shiny steel towards its thumping vein and I touched it. The goat kicked and fluttered, making me jump and fall backward into the mud, again.

I lost. I was too afraid. I couldn't do it.

I dropped the knife and ran into the house and hid under my bed. From there, breathing waves into the hanging sheet, I listened as the blood choking screams of that damned goat screeched through my bedroom window, until it went silent.

It wasn't long before I could hear my father's heavy footsteps thrashing through the house.

"Where's that little bitch?" He shouted. "I'm not going to raise some sissy little girl! He's going to learn how to be a man, and, damn it, if it's the last thing I do, I swear to God, I'm going to be the one to teach him!"

I could hear him over my poor mother's weak pleas as he stormed through the house to my bedroom door....

That night, we had goat for dinner. And that night my father asked me if I wanted to be his prissy little daughter or his chin-high, tough, and powerful son.

Goddammit, Doc... He called me *daddy's little girl*... as he raped me out in the woodshed.

· · · · ·

No, I don't want to talk about it. I don't *need* to talk about it.

Well, I don't care if that's what we're here to do. It's over with. It's done. I've moved on.

You know what? Let's talk about you. Why are **you** here, Doc? What happened in **your** life that was so traumatizing that you decided to become a therapist? Did your daddy touch you? Did your parents beat you 'til you bled? Did you watch someone die? Maybe a family member... your poor little old grandmother, perhaps? An uncle? A sibling? Which is it, Doc? Apparently, *something* had to happen to make you give a damn about us, about me.

Here's the thing about you people. You come in here in your fancy clothes, sit in your fancy chair at your fancy desk, nodding your disgusting head up and down like you know exactly what I'm thinking – like you know exactly what I've been through. Well, screw you, Doc! You don't know me! You don't have the right to judge me! Who the hell do you think you are? You're not God. You're just some piece of shit sissy who wants to talk and hug it out. Well, guess what... life doesn't work like that. It's not all unicorns and rainbows... It's blood and mud, it's death and struggle... it's **pain**! Doc, it's God damned *pain*!

Draw my anger? What the hell are you talking about?

Here, give me that. Yeah, sure, I'll draw my anger... Here, it's for you, a big middle finger... I call it, *Doc*.

Wow! You're right, that is therapeutic. I feel so much better, now. Shit, I think I'm healed. Thanks, Doc.

I'm going to go have a cigarette.

• • • • •

Alright, look. I apologize.

You're just trying to do your job. You're just trying to help. I get that. You're a good man, Doc.

Honestly, I know that I have some anger issues. I know that I tend to take it out on those around me. Yes, sometimes that means my family. But it doesn't mean that I don't love them. I love them very much. I do. I just want what's best for them. You know?

I want to give them the things that I didn't have growing up: A big TV in their room, a new computer, fancy clothes, food, and a roof over their heads.

I just want them to be strong. They need to learn and understand that the driving force of the universe is *power*. It's everything. And if they don't understand how to use that power, or how to grab power by the throat and own it, then, I'm afraid... well, I'm afraid that my kids will grow up to be victims. I'm afraid that they will be taken advantage of, lose, and become unsuccessful.

Look, I'm just trying to teach them the best way that I know how.

You get that, don't you? It's logical. It's rational. It's not insane to crave that for your kids. And they are *my* kids. I have every right to raise them in the way that I see fit. **No one** is going to tell me differently!

Call me hardheaded, old-school, a stubborn ass... I don't care. I know what works. I know what will make my kids tough. I know how to make them strong, and they will **need** to be strong if they want to get anywhere in *this* life.

The best thing that my father ever did for me was to teach me at a young age just how dangerous this world can be. He taught me that this environment is hostile and not to get too comfortable.

Complacency kills. That's what he said. *Get comfortable, and you become a victim.* I've learned that where you find happiness, you find weakness. That's just the truth. That's just the horrible, ugly, spit-in-your-face truth....

I think he was a *good* man, a decent man, my father. Yeah, sure... his unorthodox ways were controversial. But, I'll be damned if they didn't work. Look at me. I'm married with three beautiful kids, tough kids. I'm doing well in the department, earning medals and merits, building a hefty pension, as well as a reputation for putting bad guys behind bars.

Yes, I have a temper. But a man *needs* a temper. A man *needs* to be feared.

I definitely feared my father, and rightfully so. He had a heavy fist and a swift foot. He was full of hammer and nails. He was a man of action. He taught by *doing*. That was just his way. But, he got things done. Now, I'm not saying that he was an angel, or that he was perfect, no. But, to his credit, he accomplished what he set out to do....

I mean, just look at what he created. I'm a product of him, of his grit and whip. I **am** my father's son.

Look, I love my kids, Doc. I'm their father. I created them. I built them. They have my DNA, little bits of me attached all over them. They will carry on my legacy, my good name. Yes, I love them very much, and no school teacher, judge, *therapist*, or anyone else is going to say otherwise. The bond between a father and his children is sacred, it's pure, natural... Godly. No system, no man-made system can break that bond.

You know, ever since this whole misunderstanding started, ever since the first accusations were thrown at my good name, I can't help but think about when they were little. Just, these little, tiny bundles of joy... I can remember the first time that I held Ally. She was wrapped so tight in her swaddle, she looked like a small screaming burrito. I remember the sound of her laughter when I called her *my little burrito*. "I'm going to eat you," I'd joke with her, putting her tiny, soft hands into my mouth. She'd just smile the biggest smile, so sweet, so beautiful, so... stimulating.

Lately, I've had a lot of lonely hours to reflect on some of my favorite memories of their youth. It's the little things that you remember the most, Doc. I don't care how big of a deal something is, or how much planning goes into it, it's the little things that stick with you.

I remember the birthday parties... not individually, I mean, they were all mostly the same, anyway... family, friends, food, cake, and a house full of laughter and smiles. It was **happiness.** I remember their smiles, each one of their ornery, missing teeth, ear to ear, wide, grinning smiles. That's the meat on the bones, that's the sustenance, that's the charge, that's the spark that keeps an old man's heart beating.

Specifically, I remember one birthday party at our house. Another one, full of friends and family – my brother, some guys from the department, some of Ashley's old college friends – I don't recall whose party it was, but Tyler couldn't have been more than four or five years old.

We were all packed into our newly remodeled house, *we were putting in a finished basement*, and you could still smell the sawdust when you opened the basement door. Personally, I never cared for the smell of sawdust, it's... it's heavy and reminds me of small spaces... almost as if it were suffocating me. Actually, I remember having a strict rule that we were to keep the basement door shut at all times during the renovation. But, it was mostly finished, and despite my pleas for people to not go down there, someone must have, because I found the door cracked open while walking down the hall, to my office, and smelling that heavy, wet, choking, sawdust pouring up from the basement.

There was a cautious panic in Ashley's eyes when she came rushing into the office, interrupting my brother and I sharing stories of our childhood shenanigans to ask me if I had seen Tyler anywhere.

I calmly took a sip from my fresh glass of Jim Beam. "No. I don't think so. I thought he was with you?"

Her shoulders dropped, and she wiped her bangs from her eyes. "No. I've been passing out cake and ice cream for the last fifteen minutes. You haven't seen him at all?"

I distinctly remember the concerned look on my brother's face as I glanced his way, but he shook his head. "Nope. We've been in here for a little while now. Did you look out back?"

"Not yet. I thought he was with you. Okay. I'll go look outside. Could you just… look around inside for me?"

With drink in hand, I quickly followed her out the door.

It's that *feeling* that I remember so vividly. You know, all the things that are running through your head: *Is he hurt? Did he run off? Did he fall down the steps? Is he in the pond?*

Even now it still makes me shake to think about his tiny, lifeless body, floating face down in the pond out back. A place where we would kill those summer evenings, trying to catch more than just trees and grass.

I must have been sipping my drink rather quickly because, by the time I made my rounds on the second level, I was empty. So, I made my way to the kitchen to pour myself another drink. Look, I'll admit it… I had a small drinking problem back then. But it was just the stress of my job, you know.

I was in the kitchen, tipping up the bottle of Jim Beam and splashing the last of it onto shrinking ice. I had my back to the hallway when I heard the basement door creak open. I turned around just in time to suck in that awful sawdust smell.

My God, I don't know how long he was down there, but when Tyler carefully stepped into the kitchen in nothing but his t-shirt, I knew something was wrong.

He reached out with his little hand, trying to show me something that he was holding… and just as vivid and as awful as if it had happened this morning, I can still see his tight, shaking fist reaching out for me and squeezing his blood-soaked, batman underwear.

SEVEN.
THE SYSTEM

2017, October - 2018, April

Nikki, the last student to exit the classroom, paused at the door, looked back at Mrs. V. and grinned.

"See you later, Mrs. V."

Mrs. V. looked up from organizing the scattered papers on her desk and offered a heartfelt smile in return.

"You have a wonderful evening, Nikki. See you tomorrow."

"Yeah, if you're lucky." Nikki's face lit up with a big toothy smile.

Nikki's smile faded while the breeze from her exit fluttered the "Student of the Week" pictures on her sixth-grade classroom door. In place of her smile was disappointment. She shifted her book bag on her right shoulder and started down the hall towards the rumble of excited pre-teens rushing out towards freedom, towards adventure, towards home.

Nikki paused under the dim, red, exit sign and turned to look back at Mrs. V.'s door, still open, still available, still possible for her to walk back into and confess everything wrong in her life to the one person who has given her the most hope.

She filled her lungs with doubt and blew it out through the heavy doors into the cool fall air. She deflated at the sight of the big, bright busses waiting in a single file line to bump her back to the shade of Lost Road and the shadows of her white, country ranch home.

Mrs. V. sat at her large wooden desk with her light blue sweater draped over her elegant shoulders. Her thin dark hair played at the corners of her red-rimmed glasses. In front of her, a stack of sixth-grade handwritten papers waited to be graded. Her desk was organized and tidy. She had a stack of lesson books in the far right corner, and an assignment tray in the far left. Between them sat a box of tissues, hand sanitizer, and a bowl of chocolate kisses. All of which she allowed her students to help themselves to as they came into class, just as long as the trash made it into the trashcan and not onto the floor, or in their neighbor's hair.

The students had all left for the day in a hurried wave of middle school gossip and laughter. Mrs. V. was left alone in the silence of an occasional door closing and the whistle of the old custodian pushing his cart of cleaning supplies down the hallway. She loved these first few moments after a stressful day, where she could clear her head and reflect on the faces that sat in front of her all day long, like empty coin jars collecting loose change throughout the year; she loved to fill them to the brim. But, this was her quiet opportunity to read through their work, grade their assignments, and prepare for the next day. She absolutely loved it. She loved to see the progress that her students were making, and she loved to read what their wild imaginations had created.

In her right hand, between her crimson and chipped fingernail polish, she held a red ink pen. With her head bent, and rubbing her neck with her left hand, she squinted to make out Jake's sloppy handwriting. He was raving about soldiers making sacrifices to protect the rights and freedoms of the American people. She drew a straight red line though Jake's attempted spelling of the word *courageous* and wrote the proper spelling just above it.

She paused, leaned back in her big, creaking chair, and smiled at the thought of her own husband's military service. He was a marine who had endured two tours in Afghanistan with only one year in between. She remembered how she felt reading his sloppy and sweat-stained letters at the dining room table, the evening news reporting local crime and the War on Terror progress in the background, hoping that she would catch a glimpse of him or his unit. She hated that he had to be away so much, but her whole body warmed with pride whenever she would talk about him to the other teachers in the breakroom, whenever they would ask.

She brushed the hair from her mid-thirties, aging and lining face, and flipped over Jake's story about courage into the "already read" pile. She looked at the neat and tiny name at the top of the next paper: *Nikki Handler*. Mrs. V. let out a soft chuckle at how often Nikki would stay after class just to chat about her day, or lesson, or what her father had bought her that week; anything at all just to spend some time with her favorite teacher.

As the rumble of the last bus leaving faded away down the street, Mrs. V. began to read Nikki's paper. Still grinning about Nikki's quick wit and jokes, she read through the first few lines quickly. However, her grin soon turned to confusion and then concern as she read deeper into her story. She dropped her grading pen and picked Nikki's paper up off the desk for a closer look. Mrs. V. read her story about sexual abuse twice before letting the paper fall back to her desk. She removed her glasses and rubbed at her aching head. Her eyes darted around the room searching for answers.

Then, all at once, everything began to make sense: why Nikki was so excited to be at school, why she would stay after class just to talk with Mrs. V., how some days she seemed weaker than others, sick, cold, clouded... defeated. Mrs. V. sucked in the suddenly cold and shaky air and raised her trembling hand to her gaping mouth. In one furious raging wave of reality, she was overcome with tears.

That next morning, Mrs. V. didn't greet Nikki with a smile, but with a hug instead. Her soft brown eyes were full of compassion as she asked Nikki to stay and eat lunch in class with her.

"Are you serious?" Nikki's excitement was hardly contained.

"Well, sure. Why not? I'd love to hear more about your week. You know, the usual... about how you and Trisha are doing, about your brother and sister, how your mom's doing... and your *dad*."

Standing in front of her teacher's desk still holding onto her books, Nikki let her eyes drop to the floor. She could sense that something was different this time. She could feel the softness, the pity, and the worry in Mrs. V.'s voice. For a moment, she was overwhelmed with fear. For a moment, her legs nearly let go of her. It was her mind that was most active, and her thoughts ran wild at the sound of just two words: **your dad.**

My dad? Why? We don't talk about him any other time. What do I say? Should I tell her the truth? Can I tell her the truth? What will she think? What will she say? What will happen? Will I be in trouble? Will she hate me? Oh God, I don't want her to hate me.

Mrs. V. absorbed her body language. Nikki's scrunched brows and slightly moving lips standing in front of her desk. Her eyes shifting to the ground and biting at her lip. Nikki had a range of emotions playing out, vividly, across her face, like one of those old silent films that Mrs. V.'s grandmother had projected onto the wall after passing around homemade popcorn to a living room full of excited grandkids. It was Nikki's face that sounded the alarm, for Nikki wore her feelings loudly, like her favorite pair of Chuck Taylor's.

"Everything alright?

There was a long, silent pause before Nikki answered.

"Yeah..."

"*Everything?*" Mrs. V. pressed.

Nikki gazed out the window at the leaves starting to change. The reds, yellows, and oranges mixed with the pale greens. She watched them flutter in the light October breeze, shake free, and float down softly to the browning grass.

"How are things at home, Nikki? How are things with your father?"

Nikki's lip began to quiver. Her mouth started to water. Her body was letting loose. Her eyes darted away from Mrs. V. and toward the filing cabinet decorated with a rainbow of sticky notes. They formed a collage of each student's favorite new word: *abundant, immense, superior, anxious, treacherous, fortitude... courageous.*

Nikki's mind was a foray of thoughts. *What do I say? What do I say?!*

Mrs. V. was struggling herself. All she wanted to do was take this beautiful little girl into her arms, hold her, and tell her that everything was going to be okay.

She could feel her body start to shake as she set Nikki's story in front of her.

Nikki looked down at it. It wasn't hard to miss. At the top, in big, bold, red letters was the word **COURAGE**.

She finally looked at Mrs. V., hoping that it would help her words to be more convincing.

"Fine. It's... everything is... everything... is... ***not*** fine!"

Nikki could feel a warm rush and tingle in the back of her throat. She tried to swallow them down, to hold them in, but she couldn't, her emotions had been building for far too long, and they were ready to erupt.

Her books slipped from her weakening hands and crashed to the floor. And just as sudden, just as violent, and just as loud, her tears burst free from deep inside of her. She covered her face with her hands and sobbed into them. Mrs. V., suddenly crying too, rushed around her desk and took Nikki into her arms, wrapping her in warmth, in safety, and in love.

"Oh, Nikki! I'm so sorry. I'm so sorry!" She cried.

They held each other, sobbing together until they were exhausted. Then, Nikki told her everything. Nikki explained how her father has been abusing her mother, about his raging and painful temper, about how her sister seemed to hate her, and that her mother was always sad, high or drunk whenever Nikki needed her.

And to the horror of Mrs. V.'s worst imagined nightmares, Nikki described how her father forced her to touch him while everyone was sleeping.

After the tears had settled and Mrs. V. vowed to keep Nikki safe, they both lumbered through the hallway, toward the administrative office. She had convinced Nikki that she should talk with Mike and tell him everything that she had just told Mrs. V. As they walked past the decorated lockers, a tradition of the Jr. High football cheerleaders, Nikki read the bold words on their handmade signs, *Courage. Strength. Victory.* Blurring closer and closer to that black and white OFFICE sign sticking out over the top of the entrance, Nikki could feel the courage fleeing from her twisting stomach.

She reached up and grabbed Mrs. V's hand. Startled, Mrs. V. glanced down quickly to see Nikki's blue eyes staring up at her. She offered a warm smile and gently squeezed her hand.

"It'll be alright, Nikki. I promise."

Nikki's loud breathing was drowned out by the lunchroom noise as they approached the office. They stopped outside of the big glass door that led into the central office which housed several administrative offices, a supply room, and the copy machine that Mrs. V. sometimes sent Nikki to use for class assignments.

"Will you come in with me?" Nikki asked.

Mrs. V. thought for a moment about her lunch and class schedule.

"Of course I will."

"Will you sit beside me while I talk to him?"

"Honey, I don't know if I'm allowed to stay in there or not. It might be against school policy."

"Please?" Nikki's begging practically broke Mrs. V.'s heart.

"I tell you what, I promise to do everything that I am able to do. How does that sound?"

"Do you swear?"

"I swear."

"Pinky swear?" Nikki let out a soft chuckle.

Mrs. V. smiled, "Pinky swear."

She held open the door for Nikki and motioned to the secretary that they were heading to the back offices.

Standing outside Mike's closed door, Nikki grabbed her hand again. Mrs. V. pat it softly.

"I'm right here. Be brave. Be courageous. Be you."

Nikki bit her lip in thought, and with one deep breath, she reached out and knocked loudly on Mike's door.

• • • • •

Mrs. V. had been in Mike's office for nearly five minutes when they both finally opened the door and invited Nikki inside to discuss the story she wrote and the horrors that she unveiled to Mrs. V.

Ashley had arrived in a confused panic. She was sitting at home sipping wine and reading one of her books about beach love stories, which she desperately wished would become a reality for her, when the school called and advised her that she needed to come in right away because of Nikki. As she greeted Mike, he informed her that Nikki had some trouble at home and they would all like to discuss it. Now, sitting in the corner opposite of Mrs. V., her gut nearly came undone at the thought of what that "trouble" could be.

Nikki sat in Mike's purple chair as he listened patiently, compassionately, and empathetically to her story about Haley, knowing all along that her story was a way for her to reach out for help. So, he tread lightly, gently, doing his best to encourage her along the way. At first, she was scared. She only read him the story she wrote about Haley and hoped that he would see right through it. With a little encouragement, she admitted that the story was about **her**, not Haley. Then, like she opened up to Mrs. V., she opened up to Mike and told him what her father had done to her and her mother. She only hesitated at the most difficult parts, when Mike would ask about the details, those sharp, rusty, jagged details that would rip open an old wound each time.

Mike had sat at his desk with his hands folded, scowling at the ugliest parts and holding back his own emotions when Nikki would tear up. He had been taught to listen objectively, to set aside his own agendas, his own skeletons, his own biases, and to read his client's body language, to hear the tone in their voice, to seek out the truth. He had learned over the years what types of questions to ask and what sort of advice to give. But even after all of his experience as a therapist, it had never become routine, it had never become less appalling while listening to another sexual assault victim reveal to him their horrors and agony. Quite frankly, it enraged him. It lit his soul on fire, made his palms sweat, his teeth grit, and his muscles flex. He wanted nothing more than to save these children, to rescue them from the torments of their demons. He wanted to be their hero, and some days he was. But the truth was, Mike always felt like his hands were tied, that policy kept him from doing his best work. He felt that the system was flawed, and he spent the second half of his career, trying to change it.

Now, more than ever, Mike yearned to make a difference. He ached to wipe Nikki's pain away as he watched her sorry eyes cry and try to explain the abominations that were going on in her home.

But, Nikki was brave. Nikki was a warrior, a fighter, a survivor; and Mike soon realized that she was even stronger than he could ever be.

"Nikki, you've been so courageous, today. I want you to know that. It takes real courage to talk about the things we just did. Thank you for being so brave."

Nikki wiped a slow tear from her cheek with a tissue that Mike had offered her.

"I just want it to end. I want it all to be over. I just want my daddy to love me."

That comment shot an arrow straight through Mike's heart. He swallowed down the emotions, but his eyes were beginning to wet.

Ashley just shook her head in disbelief and anger. Her right hand was wrapped around a wadded tissue, which she realized she was squeezing into a fist as her left hand wiped at the tears rolling down her face. She didn't utter a word. It was too late for talk. No matter how hard she tried to shake it, she could only blame herself. *How could I have let this happen? What kind of mother am I? Maybe the kids would be better off without me?*

Mrs. V. was sobbing in the corner, quietly. She offered as much of a smile as she could muster when Nikki turned to look at her.

"Thanks for staying with me, it really helped to have you here."

Mrs. V. nodded, "Oh, Nikki…"

There was a pause, a moment of awkward silence, a moment for them all to digest the sour details and to figure out what to do next.

Mike leaned back in his rolling chair and rubbed at his chin.

"By law, I have to contact the police."

"The police?" Nikki's fear was obvious.

"I know, given the circumstances of who your father is and what he's done for this town, I know that it won't be easy, but we must get them involved. That's how these things are handled. That's the way to justice."

Nikki looked back at Mrs. V. who gave an affirming nod. Then to her mother, who was still wiping tears away. When Ashley saw her daughter's puffy blue eyes, she knew that she had to hold her. Ashley jutted up from her chair, rushed her daughter, picked her up and held her tightly while they shared lasting tears.

After a short while, Mike shifted forward in his chair. "Nikki, I'll be right here with you the whole time. It'll be alright. We're all here for you, to help you, to support you, and to protect you. I promise."

In the jittery thirty minutes it took for the two police officers to arrive, Mrs. V. had returned to class, but not before hugging Nikki and whispering how proud she was of her and her bravery. Nikki sat with Mike working on a crossword puzzle in the local newspaper. Ashley sat rubbing her back for a while, trying to comfort her as best she could. She had excused herself to the lady's room to cry alone when finally, the police arrived.

"Good afternoon, Mike." Officer Barnes shook Mike's hand.

Officer Swine merely lifted his chin in Mike's direction before taking out his notepad and pen.

"So, what seems to be the problem here?" Officer Barnes asked.

Mike's eyes shifted towards Nikki.

"Hey, aren't you Jim's daughter?" Officer Swine asked Nikki.

Surprised by his recognition, Nikki hesitated.

"Yes. Yes, sir, I am."

Officer Swine tapped Officer Barnes on the shoulder and laughed.

"Hey, you remember that one time when Jim brought in those drunks who were fighting in the Sheetz parking lot? Remember when the one dark fella tried to run out the front door, handcuffed and all? And Jim jumped his desk, ran him down, and dragged him back in all bloody and cursing?"

Officer Barnes laughed out loud. "Honey, your father is a legend around here." He shifted his duty belt, and a clear reminiscing smile spread across his face. Mike cleared his throat and brought both officers back to business.

"So, what happened? Was there a fight?" Officer Barnes quickly looked her over with his flashlight for any marks or blood.

Officer Swine stood by studying Nikki's sad and scared face.

"Are you getting bullied? Is that what this is about? Dispatch said something about an assault?" He leaned down to meet her eye level. "I don't stand for any kind of bullying. I was bullied in school, too. I ended up having to fight back just to get him to leave me alone. It's ok. Tell me what happened."

Mike shifted uncomfortably standing by his desk. He knew that this would not be easy. He knew what kind of status Mr. Handler has in the community. But he was also certain that this was the right thing to do. He was determined to save this little girl, regardless of what anyone else thought about her father.

"Well, we need to report a crime. A... domestic assault... a... *sexual* assault." Mike's tone slapped the smile from the officer's face.

"Sexual assault? At home?" Officer Barnes asked Nikki who slowly shook her head up and down.

"By *who*? You're brother? One of his friends?" Officer Swine's tone was the least bit empathetic, but rather, confrontational.

"Her father," Mike interjected.

Officer Swine chuckled in disbelief.

"Jim? Get out of here. Jim Handler? No way?"

Officer Barnes shot Officer Swine a look that made him snap back to professionalism.

Officer Barnes leaned down to her level, closer and softer this time.

"Dear, you–"

"My name... is Nikki," she said firmly.

Taken aback, Officer Barnes raised his hat and studied Nikki's face.

"Sorry. *Nikki*, you *do* know it's against the law to make false reports, right?"

This made Nikki's jaw drop. Her eyes filled with anger as she glanced up at Mike who was leaning against his desk. Mike crossed his arms and puffed out his chest, a thing he catches himself doing when trying to look authoritative.

"Look, Officer Barnes, this is a serious matter which requires your serious professionalism and attention. Can we please get on with it?"

Officer Barnes and Officer Swine looked at each other and then at Mike.

"My apologies, Mike. Needless to say, I'm a little caught off guard, here. Could you please give us just a minute?" Officer Barnes asked.

"Uh. Okay. Take your time, gentlemen," Mike said sarcastically as he offered Nikki a peppermint lifesaver from the secret stash in his top desk drawer. She took it and rolled her eye in the officers' general direction as they exited Mike's office and stepped into the other room.

Officer Swine looked around to make sure no one could hear him.

"Look, Ronnie, I don't know about this, it just doesn't add up," he said, crossing his arms.

"Yeah, I don't like it either, Nick. But we have to do our jobs. We need to file a report. There's no trying to sweep this thing under the rug. You understand?"

Officer Swine removed his hat and rubbed at his forehead.

"Well, what if we call Jim down here? Maybe her story will change in front of him."

Officer Barnes shook his head as he thought.

"No. I don't like that. We can't have the perpetrator and victim in the same room as we interview them."

"But it's Jim. Come on. How long have you known him? Fifteen... twenty years?" Wouldn't you want that courtesy if you were in his position?"

"Well..." Officer Barnes sucked in deeply and let it out loudly. "Five minutes. We'll give him five minutes in there to tell his side of things and see if her story changes. Five minutes, Nick. That's it. I'm serious."

"Oh, I'm sure her story will change. I'd bet my job on it. There's no way that Jim could do something so... disgusting."

"After this, it's by the book. You got it? We don't need any kind of scene down here at the school. Okay?"

"Alright, I'll give him a call. Let's hear him out."

Officer Swine opened up his phone, rifled through his contacts and gave Jim a call.

The officers walked back into Mike's office to see that Ashley had returned from the restroom.

"Hello, Ashley. It's good to see you, again. Although, I wish it were under other circumstances." Officer Barnes said. "Officer Swine just got off the phone with Jim, he's on his way over here so that we can straighten this out."

Ashley's jaw dropped. Mike's head snapped up from his notes.

"What? Are you out of your mind? This isn't the policy procedure! This is absurd!" Mike said furiously.

"Just calm down, Mike," said Officer Barnes. "We just want to get to the bottom of this. That's all."

Ashley threw out her hands. "How is that going to help the situation? You need to arrest him! Not invite him down here for tea and cookies!"

"Arrest him?" Officer Swine laughed. "How about you let us do our job first, Ma'am." He said coldly. "Now, Nikki, how about you tell us what happened? Every detail."

Nikki was reliving the details for the third time, at the request of officer Swine, when Jim burst through the door with the school secretary close behind.

"Jim! Jim!" She shouted, "I said wait until I ring you in. Mike, I'm so sorry. He just came rushing in."

Mike held up his hand and nodded to Mrs. Wright. "Thank you. We'll handle it from here."

Jim offered a warm smile and handshake to both officers. He tried to hug Ashley, but she refused. With a genuinely concerned face, he gravitated toward Nikki. But, his concern was more for himself than for her.

"What happened, Nik? Are you okay? Did someone hurt you? Who was it? I'll bust their skull open!"

Ashley couldn't hold back her anger any longer. "You son of a bitch! You sick, sick, son of a bitch." She stormed Jim in an angry rush of wild slaps to the head.

Both officers pulled her off of Jim and took her out to the other room to calm down. They came back in and locked the door behind them.

"Uhhh, Jim... I uh, I don't know how to say this exactly," Said Officer Barnes.

Officer Swine interrupted. "You daughter is accusing you of sexually assaulting her. Could you talk some sense into her, please?"

"This is absurd!" Mike shouted. "What the hell's going on here?"

"Now, calm down, Mike," Officer Barnes insisted, "Let us do our job."

"Your *job*? Your job is to protect this young lady from this man! But, here you are, bringing them face to face, let alone in my office. This is insane!"

"Mike," Jim was on his knee beside Nikki with his hand on her leg, squeezing it tight enough to let her know that she had better keep her mouth shut. She was shooting flames and daggers at him from both eyes, "Listen, let's just keep our cool, alright. Or we're going to have to ask you to leave so that you don't upset my daughter."

"*Leave?* This is **my** office, if anyone is leaving, it will be **you!**"

Officer Barnes held up his hands.

"Alright! Alright, everybody. Let's just take a second to breathe. Jim, you want to explain your side of the story here?"

"My side of the story?" Jim stood up. "I haven't done anything but give my family everything that they've ever wanted."

Nikki looked down at the floor and shook her head. She didn't know whether to kick this man in the leg and run, or just give in and accept that she would always be his victim.

"All I've ever done is spoil her." Jim started to stroke her hair, but she pulled away quickly.

"Don't touch me! Get away from me!" She growled.

Jim pulled her against his chest, holding her still, hugging her, pressuring her.

She tried to push him away. Jim tried to calm her down.

"It's ok, Nikki. It's alright. Whatever happened, it's over now."

"No! Get off me! Stop! Quit touching me!" She screamed.

Mike had enough. He took an aggressive couple of steps toward Jim.

"Let her go, Jim!"

With his attention at Mike, Nikki saw her chance. She reached up and raked her fingernails down his face. He let go, shocked.

"You're not going to touch me anymore!" Nikki became hysterical.

Jim reached out for her as Mike reached out for Jim. Nikki reared back and swung at Jim, smacking him across the face, turning his cheek a stinging red and leaving his mouth gaping open. She shattered into tears as Mike shoved Jim away from her.

Officer Swine jumped in front of Jim, more protecting him than holding him back. Officer Barnes grabbed Nikki and cradled her in the opposite corner.

"Alright, get him out of here, Nick." Officer Barnes took charge of the room. "It's ok, honey. It's alright. Calm down, it's over. He's leaving."

"Sorry, Jim. I got to take you outside." Officer Swine opened the door. Jim looked at him, at Nikki, Mike, and then at Officer Barnes.

"You gotta be kiddin' me."

Then, he walked out on his own, passed the hissing eyes of his wife, out into a burning sun and to the back of the police cruiser. Officer Swine opened the rear door and politely asked Jim to get inside.

• • • • •

Judge Norman sat in his chambers twisting his gray mustache between his finger and thumb while looking over the evidence of a very quick and quiet investigation. At his large rosewood desk, and still in his black robe, he wrestled with the idea of sentencing a local hero.

To his rear, hanging on the wall, was a large picture of Thomas Jefferson. Around his chambers were remanence of a simpler time. Mounted on an Ohio State shaped plaque to his right, he sported the big twelve-point buck that he shot on his brother's farm, and above that was an old English musket of which he was the winning bid for at the Mayor's nephew's cancer benefit over at the VFW. To his left stood both the American and Ohio State flag. Presented on a stand directly beneath them was a picture of Judge Norman in his Army fatigues, posing with his rifle in front of an Apache helicopter. In the center of the room was a large bear rug; a brown bear that he bagged in Alaska on a hunting trip of a lifetime when his father was diagnosed with cancer. On the mantle above his bookcase were a seventeen-year-old bottle of scotch and two whiskey glasses. His desk was decorated with a picture of his family, an autographed baseball from Pete Rose, and an antler-handled letter opener laying on top of a pile of envelopes.

He leaned back in his old groaning chair, reading over the police reports and statements from Jim's family. For him, personally, it was extremely difficult to visualize Jim Handler doing anything remotely close to the accusations that were brought against him by his youngest daughter. He grew to know Jim very well over the years, from several big drug busts to kidnappings, armed robberies, and of course The Wills Creek Massacre. Jim had proven himself to be a reliable, honest, trustworthy, and respectable enforcer of the law, as well as a good friend. Jim was on Judge Norman's championship softball team, played host to many parties and cookouts, and would even drop off a bottle of Jack Daniels during the Christmas season.

Judge Norman read over part of Nikki's statement one more time:

Sometimes dad gets really angry after work. Those are the bad days. Those are the days where we try to avoid him. He takes it out on mom, mostly. We can hear it from our bedrooms. His yelling and cursing, his hand smacking across mom's face, it echoes up the stairway and down the hall into our rooms.

Mom doesn't fight back. I don't know why – I guess she still loves him. But, the mornings after, I watch her powder over the bruising on her cheeks. I feel bad for her. I wish she would do something. I wish she would stand up to him.

It's usually on those nights that he's the worst. Those are the nights that he sneaks into my room. I can feel him watching me. It's like that feeling when Mrs. V. asks us to write something on the chalkboard, you can just feel all those eyes staring at you, hoping that you mess up or do something funny, so that they can laugh at you. That's kind of how it feels when he's standing outside my door watching me. I think he's trying to see if I'm awake or not.

Those nights... he touches me. Those nights...he makes me touch him. The first time, about a year ago, I had no idea what was happening. I thought it was... normal. But it didn't feel normal. It felt wrong. It felt so... so... wrong.

He said that if I told anyone, he would deny it. He said that he would take it out on Mom. He said that he would beat her until she couldn't talk. I don't know if he was serious or just trying to scare me, but it worked for a long time.

Dad told me that if I was a good girl, he would buy me whatever I wanted. So, I did what I was told. I let him touch me, and I touched him back. Then he would buy me new shoes, a TV, clothes, toys... anything that I asked for. He did that with all of us.

Those were the good days. When he would take us shopping. It was almost as if it wasn't wrong anymore, it almost felt right. We would laugh and talk about how our days have been. He would buy us snacks and candy. He would tell us how much he loved us and that he would never let anyone hurt us.

*I don't know if he realized that **he** was the one that was hurting us.*

Judge Norman tossed the file onto his desk. He was mentally in a hard place as he realized that there was not enough evidence to convict Jim of sexual assault. It was another case of *her* word versus *his*, and he figured the whole town would have his head if he tried to criminalize their hero in a public forum. He could see it now, protests and disorder, angry citizens crucifying him for tarnishing their hero. Not to mention, it was an election year. He was aware that he had to please the masses if he wished to be re-elected. He wanted this all to go away. He wanted it gone, off his desk, to disappear like that drug dealer who sold his nephew that heroin. He even thought about sweeping it under the rug. But, the moral side of his conscience wouldn't allow that to happen.

He paged his bailiff.

"John. John, could you bring them in, please?"

"Yes, sir, judge."

The bailiff escorted Jim's defense lawyer and the prosecuting lawyer into Judge Norman's office.

The defense lawyer, an enthusiastic young man fresh out of law school, dressed in a flashy black suit and thin-rimmed glasses, attempted to shake Judge Norman's hand.

The Judge glanced at his outstretched hand and then quickly up into the young man's optimistic eyes.

"Have a seat, son."

The prosecuting lawyer, a man in his forties with nearly twenty years under his belt, snickered at his young counterpart's inexperience with whom the people called, *No Nonsense Judge Norman*.

"Gentlemen, we have ourselves a bit of a situation on our hands, now don't we?"

"Well, sir, my client is clearly innocent, and I can prove it."

"Son, I can appreciate your luster, but after reading his little girl's statement, not to mention all of the others, I'm not so sure that you can prove, beyond a reasonable doubt, that Jim is innocent. And, damn it, that pains me more to acknowledge than you realize."

He leaned back and turned his chair sideways to look up at the picture of Jefferson hanging behind his desk. He hardly noticed it as much as he used to. Back then, he tried to imagine exactly what America's Forefathers had in mind when they created this *free nation*.

He whipped back around to face them and slapped his hands on his desk.

"But, on the other hand, the evidence is more *his* story vs. *their* story. To be blunt, I'm not quite sure that we have enough here for the case to be substantiated."

Without another word, Judge Norman got up and walked over to the bottle of scotch on his mantle. He pointed it in their direction, an offer that each of them declined with a short rattle of their heads.

He puffed.

"Well, I need a drink."

The Judge poured himself a heavy shot in a whiskey glass engraved with

No Nonsense Judge Norman, a Christmas gift from his long-time bailiff, John, and downed it with one gasping swallow. Then, he carried them over to his desk, pounding the bottle to the old worn-down wood like his gavel in the courtroom just outside the door to his left.

"I don't like this one bit. It smells like potpourri in a shithouse, it just doesn't make sense. It's trouble, gentlemen. Damned trouble for all involved: you, me, our beloved little town... Jim."

He poured a little more in his glass and took a sip.

The prosecuting attorney cleared his throat.

"Well sir, we are ready to go to trial if we have to, but quite honestly, I think it would be in everyone's best interest to settle this one by other means."

Jim's attorney sat straight up. "By other means?"

Judge Norman looked disgusted as he swirled his glass. "He means a plea deal."

"Now wait just a minute, here! My client isn't guilty of anything more than acting as a strong disciplinarian with a bit of a temper and a whole lot of emotion. That's it! He's been under a lot of stress lately. Judge, he's an innocent man... he's innocent of these *ridiculous* sexual assault accusations!"

Judge Norman finished his drink in a quick head tilt back and slammed his glass beside the bottle.

"You both know what will happen if this thing goes to trial. We'll have the media up all of our asses. It'll be national news. They'll dig up dirt on every single one of us and twist it however they like, just for a story. This town will get a black eye. Do you want that? Well, I sure in the hell don't. I've worked too damn hard to have some punk journalist start smearing my name, my family, my friends, my law enforcement... **my town.**"

He turned to look out of his second-story window across the town square. A few people were walking casually down the sidewalk, an elderly couple greeted a young man in a blue football jersey selling raffle tickets outside the local bakery, where everyone gets their morning doughnuts and birthday cakes. He saw Mr. Smith carrying another box of presumed snacks, baby wipes, tobacco, and energy drinks to the post office, another care package gathered at the Stop Nine Church of Christ for his son overseas in Afghanistan.

He shook his head.

"I won't have it! Damn it, I won't let that happen!"

He turned back around towards the prosecuting attorney.

"What do you have for me?"

"Well, sir, to save face, and well, this town, we are willing to offer a pretty impressive deal. After all, it's Jim. We will drop all felony, and sexual assault charges down to misdemeanor simple assault and misdemeanor child endangerment. I think we can all agree that this is a fair and *just* deal considering the situation. I believe that this will allow us to not only save this town's reputation, Judge Norman but also let us quickly deal justice and move on to the more serious drug and gang-related crimes infesting our area."

Judge Norman drew in a deep breath of contemplation. Still staring out the window with his hands in his pockets and belly out, he grunted.

"Yeah. Yeah, I think I can live with that. How about you, son?" He walked back over to his seat, sat down, and extended his hand towards Jim's lawyer.

The defense lawyer stared at his hand for a moment, looked at Jim, who nodded his head. He reached out his hand with a thrust and shook Judge Norman's hand.

"I think we can all live with that. Let me confer with my client and see if I can't convince him to take this offer."

Twenty minutes later, Jim and his lawyer walked toward the defense side of the courtroom and sat down.

"All rise!"

The two attorneys and Jim stood up while Judge Norman entered the room.

"No need to sit, this will be quick," he said as he took his seat in front of them.

"Jim, I assume that your lawyer has explained the circumstances?"

"Yes, Your Honor."

"Good. Now hear this. I don't want to know whether or not you did what you've been accused of, Jim, I don't want to know. Given your reputation, your sacrifices for this city, this county, this state, I can't help but feel... well, quite frankly, pissed off. Jim, how in the hell did you get yourself in this situation? You know damn well what's expected out of our law enforcement around here. I don't know what you are dealing with, mentally. Hell, I can't imagine the nightmares you have to deal with in your line of work. But man up! You have a family, you have a reputation, you have our reputation to uphold. So, get it together. Alright?"

"Yes, Your Honor. I understand."

"Alright then. Taking into consideration your reputation among the community, your clean record, and constant dedication to serve and protect this town, here's what's going to happen. Jim— according to our plea deal, all felony and sexual assault charges are dropped. You are now faced with misdemeanor simple assault and misdemeanor child endangerment. How do you plea?"

"No contest, Your Honor."

"Okay. Then, I sentence you to one-year probation, one hundred hours of community service, three months of zero contact with the victims, and six months of therapy. That will be all. You are dismissed."

Judge Norman pounded his gavel which echoed through the courtroom.

For Jim, the reverberations were arousing as he shook off whatever restraint was left in his being. He felt free. He felt alive. He felt empowered.

"Thank you, Your Honor. Thank you, Tom." He said with a small, tight smile.

EIGHT.
THE MONSTER

2018, July - 2018, August

Mike sat at his desk in his private office, looking over the Handler's file one more time. He flipped through the pages, stopping at the highlighted sections, re-reading the trauma and abuse of each separate child, of Ashley, and of Jim's mild progress in the last three months.

Mike brushed his hand through his dark and barely gray hair. He was exhausted, mostly from worrying about Jim's re-entry into the home, but also about the fate of humanity. He looked at the picture of his wife and two daughters, standing in front of their school on graduation day last year. They looked so happy smiling, his eldest in her cap and gown, soon leaving for Ohio University. He worried about her then, but even more so now. He couldn't possibly imagine either of his daughters being sexually assaulted. It was the worst fear of any father, and he struggled with trying to understand Jim's mind, Jim's heart, and Jim's motivations. He feared for the world that he now lived in, where a justice system enabled a father to do the unthinkable to his own family, and a sleeping community that had no idea of the monster that they called "hero."

He rested his head against his hand, skimming his notes on Jim, and trying to evaluate whether or not he genuinely possessed any amount of remorse or regret. Finally, he closed the file and tossed it aside. He buried his face into his hands, rubbed at his temples, at his forehead, trying to alleviate the pain, the burden of knowing the atrocities that he knows. He massaged the bridge of his nose, squeezing out the pressure of wading through Jim's truth or bullshit. He pinched at his shoulders and neck, trying to release the weight of this case from his back. He wanted to do more. He wished he could save them all. But, all he could really offer, was to listen with empathy, to take detailed notes, to mark progress vs. regression, to give evaluated advice, to suggest tested coping skills, and to show them all that some people do truly care.

His phone intercom buzzed.

"Mike?"

"Yes?"

"The Handlers are here."

"Okay, great. Send them in, please."

"Will do."

He shuffled the papers on his desk and shoved the file into the bottom left drawer of his desk and walked over to open the door.

"Well, hello there everyone. I'm glad you all could make it. Please, come on in, have a seat, get comfortable."

"Thank you." Ashley, motioned for her children to go in and have a seat in the semi-circled cushioned chairs arranged in front of Mike's desk.

Nikki was quick to take the seat directly in front of Mike's chair. Ally and Tyler sat in the last chair at each end leaving an empty seat between them and Nikki.

Mike pulled Ashley aside.

"May I talk to you alone for a second?"

"Sure."

"Give us just a second, guys," Mike said closing the door and stepping into the hall with Ashley beside the 'Love starts with YOU!' red letters on the wall.

"How are you doing, Ashley?"

Ashley crossed her arms and leaned against the wall reading those large red letters, again.

"Fine, I guess."

"Look, are you sure that you really want to do this? Do you really want to invite him back into your home?"

Ashley sucked in a deep breath through her nose and let it out deliberately through trembling pursed lips. She looked past Mike to his door. On the outside hung a picture of a baby kitten dangling from a small branch, holding on for dear life. Above the kitten in a white oval was written in black: "Hang on! Don't let go!" Just on the other side of that, sat her children, scrolling through their phones, bored, and waiting for someone to change their future. She wanted to be that change.

"I don't know, Mike. Jim's my husband. He's their father. You don't know him like I do. You haven't seen the worthiness inside of him that I have seen. I still have hope. Besides, you said that he feels remorse. You said that he could change."

Ashley pictured Jim a few weeks ago down on his knees outside of her red Chevy blazer, after lunch, at their second favorite grill, The Cut. It was one of the places where all of their friends would get together, shoot pool, laugh, and throw a few cold ones back. But seeing him so vulnerable, so weak, so in need of her love, nearly broke her. He insisted that he was a changed man, that he still loved her and the family, and that he wanted to be a better father and husband. He convinced her that *this family could still work!* After all, there had been no talk of divorce, and as far as she was concerned, he was still her husband, *for better or for worse*, and he was still the father of her children.

"We're not getting a divorce, Mike. That's out of the question. He can still be saved. Our family can still be saved. *Wouldn't you say?* After months of therapy with all of us, isn't there still a chance for a happy ending?"

"Hmm. Yes. I want to believe that there is still a chance for happiness, for healing. You know, for him to get better. I desperately prefer to believe that. But... I just worry about you and the kids. I worry that, even after everything we have done, all the therapy and help, I worry that nothing will change." Mike rubbed at his tired neck. "The truth is, sometimes it just doesn't."

"I think, no matter the evil that he has or hasn't done... I think my kids still need a father figure. He does bring discipline to the household. You have to give him that. He holds the kids accountable. I'm pretty sure that you can agree that is something that they need, right?"

"No, I totally agree. They certainly need that. But what they don't need is more abuse. Do you think that he is capable of any more abuse?"

"I want to forgive him, Mike. I still want to hold onto the man that he used to be. I *want* this to work. I *need* my family back *together*."

Mike rubbed at his chin. Then, he scratched at the back of his head.

"I suppose I can understand that. Alright then, let's get to it."

Mike opened the door for Ashley, and she smiled at her children as she took a seat. Mike sat down in his rolling chair and scooted it up to his desk. Once comfortable, he pulled out his notepad from under a stack of files and flipped to an empty page. At the top right, he wrote the date and time. He wrote each of their names in order of age from Ashley down to Nikki at the top center of the page. The Handler family sat in silence gathering their thoughts and waiting, accustomed to this brief procedure.

Once he finished organizing his notes, Mike looked up and offered a heartfelt smile to the group.

"I just want to start by thanking you all for agreeing to meet together. I know from speaking to you individually that you all have gone through similar trauma. I think that incorporating family therapy, at least a couple times a month, will really help the healing process. Honestly, it's amazing what comfort and strength you can get from a group of people who have endured the same forms of trauma."

He paused as mental flashes of their stories played out in his head. He quickly blinked them away.

"Well, I guess the biggest issue that I'd like to tackle today would be Jim moving back into the home. What are your thoughts, concerns, stresses? What would you all like to discuss about this situation?"

Mike looked around the room waiting for any of them to respond. Ally shifted her eyes to the floor. Tyler turned his gaze to the different books on the shelf beside him, twirling the hair behind his ear, nervously. Ashley looked at her children waiting for one of them to speak up. Nikki's eyes darted back and forth from Mike to her journal sitting on her lap. When she first mentioned it in one of her sessions, Mike's face lit up with happiness, "Oh, that's wonderful!" He had said. "Journaling is such a great coping skill. I would love to see some of your journal entries. Please, *please*, bring it in with you from now on." She had used her journal as a way to share the things that she found most difficult to talk about.

Now she cleared her throat and shifted her body to get comfortable.

"Nikki?" Mike encouraged with raised eyebrows, "Would you like to get us started, today?"

She looked down at her journal.

"Well, I wrote a poem the other night about Dad coming back home. Should I read it?"

Mike folded his hands under his chin and gave her his full attention.

"Yes, please, that would be wonderful. Thank you."

Nikki opened her journal and flipped to a dog-eared page towards the back.

"Okay, well, it's not finished yet, but... but I think you'll like it."

She looked around at her family, who were all giving her their undivided attention.

"It's called, At Daddy's Hands."

At Daddy's Hands

At Daddy's Hands, I start to tremble, like a craft wood taking shape.
His rough sandpaper scratching at my thighs, rubbing, marking, etching his
name, boldly, into what he claims is his.

At Daddy's Hands, I feel no love, like what I used to feel when he would help reel
in a fish, or the times he placed his gun into my little hands and told me to shoot
at that Campbells can as if it were trying to hurt me.

At Daddy's Hands, I cry at night, trying to understand his hate.
When they used to be so soft and warm, but now sharp and hard, stabbing at my
*mind, at **me**, like a knife into flesh.*

At Daddy's Hands, I try to forgive all the pain and sorrow that strangles from
the pointy tips of his raging hands, when he seeks at night to fill his bed, with a
desire I wish would leave him dead.

• • • • • • •

While listening to his football coach give a speech about family in the locker room, Tyler faded back to a few weeks ago on the first day that his father moved back in.

"Kids, could you come down here, please?" Jim yelled up the stairs to his children who were reading, writing, and watching TV in their rooms.

Jim stood in front of the couch and his favorite chair. The blinds were open, letting the orange glow of a fading sun glare across the room. Small speckles of dust floated across the beams of stretching light. It was quiet enough to hear the faint chirping of the crickets and tree frogs. It was a perfect summer evening, Jim's first back in the home.

"Please, have a seat. Tyler, you can sit in my chair, if you'd like."

"You serious?"

"Yeah, go ahead. You've been the man of the house since I've been away. You earned it."

The girls joined Ashley, leg-tucked on the couch, and Tyler took an awkward seat in his father's chair.

Tyler looked over at his sisters, who seemed understandably nervous. "It'll be okay," he mouthed from the chair as he nodded at them. He had taken on the role of the man of the house for the last three months since his father had been gone. In those three months, he and his sisters had grown closer. Tyler had shown Nikki how to catch a football and even made it a goal of his to finally become friends with Ally's boyfriend, Brian. But now sitting in his father's chair, he couldn't help but to want to comfort them, to protect them, to let them know that he was capable of downing this monster – *if it came to that*.

Jim cleared his throat, took a drink of his ice water, and set it on the coffee table.

"Thank you. Uh… well, I'm just going to come out and say it. I'm sorry. I'm sorry for everything that I put you all through. I mean that. I honestly and sincerely mean that."

He reached for his water and took another drink. He clearly looked nervous to Tyler, who studied him, searching for clues of the truth. Tyler had learned how to read his father's body language over the last year and he caught onto Jim's nervous ticks: his rapid blinking, his eyes drifting in the upper left-hand corner when he was searching for another lie, and his thumb rubbing against his fingertips as he stretched the truth to nearly unbelievable extents. Tyler was becoming a pro at reading his father's bullshit.

But Jim had been called out on his nervous ticks in his sessions with Mike. Mike was quick and unafraid to call him out on his lying.

But Jim adapted. Just like a wild animal trying to survive, he adapted to his environment. He learned from it. He grew from it. He became skilled in it. Jim had learned how to adjust the charades that Tyler had become so good at understanding. Therapy for Jim had become a way to practice and fine-tune his art of manipulation. He had become an even better trickster, a magician, smoke and mirrors for his audiences' amusement. Jim's mental disorder had covered itself in camouflage, and his prey could not see the death trap that they were walking into.

"I know that I have hurt you all, so much. I know that I have been more of a monster than a father. But I want you all to know, right now, that I am a changed man. I am a *better* man. Honestly, therapy with Mike opened my eyes to this sickness, this… *devastation* that I have been wreaking onto my family.

He has shown me ways to change the way I think, to... to correct my thinking errors, to use my coping skills, and to stop focusing solely on *my* needs, but the needs of my family as well. I mean, after all... that *is* what we are, right... a **family?**"

Tyler thought back to that first-day speech that his father had given the family. Now, sitting in a team football meeting with his coach, hearing him preach about *this* family, about his *football family*, Tyler's arms bumped up with understanding, with fear... with shame. Tyler had wanted to believe his father's apology and willingness to change.

But that was back then, and this was now, and in the two months since his father had been home, Tyler had watched his father's slow, trembling hands transform back to rock and hammer. He had felt his father's anger across his cheek. He had heard his younger sister's sobs as she prayed to God for help. He had seen his mother slip further away into her own addiction and self-medication of booze and pills. He had witnessed his father's blatant disregard for fatherly love and compassion, and in its place, instead, boomed confidence... arrogance, a sense of comfortability realizing that he may very well get away with anything that he pleased. Jim had faced the system and won. And it had only taken him two weeks at home to reclaim his prize... his *family*.

Tyler faded in and out of his thoughts, literally shaking them away when they became too vivid. Squeezing the foam padding of the weight bench that he sat on while his coach roared inspiration throughout the locker room, in that inspiring moment he decided that, no matter what it took, he would no longer bear the curse of his father's blood. He didn't want to be anything like his father. And on that sweat-stained weight bench, he vowed to never become that monster.

"Look at one another!" Coach demanded. "This is your brother! This is your family. You are soldiers... and **that field** is our battleground. That field is *our* ground. Will you fight for it? Will you defend it? Will you count on one another when things get tough? When they go south? When shit hits the fan? Will you embrace your brother when he has made a mistake or let you down? Will you pick him up when he has fallen?"

Coach turned to his dry-erase board and wrote FAMILY in large black letters.

"Gentlemen, families look out for one another. They bleed with each other, they cry with each other, they heal with each other, and, men, they win or lose with each other!"

Tyler let his coach's speech pound into his core. He thought back to when he was almost removed from the team for his "incident." He allowed his thoughts to wander back to last year, to the "incident," and to what he did to Green Bean. He felt ashamed. He felt weak and ugly. And in that moment of terrible realization, he felt as disgusting as his father.

Tyler felt sick. With his hand over his mouth, he quickly excused himself into the restroom and vomited into the toilet. He never thought it possible that he could resemble the monster that he was born from. Beyond his worst nightmares, he never imagined that he would harm anyone else in the way that his father had harmed his family. It was this thought that ate at his soul, it rotted in his gut, and it spewed out of him in loud, groaning heaves.

The door to the bathroom swung open, and he heard a group of familiar voices heckling and laughing at a younger classman. He wiped his mouth on his shirt and flushed the toilet one last time before he stepped out of the stall. It was the starting defensive linemen, all with shaved heads, muscles bulging in their cut-off shirts, and matching stubbled faces that they thought made them look cool.

"Heyyy, Hands! There you are, just in time," Mac, the biggest and eldest of the three said grinning.

Tyler walked past him, ignoring the invite to harass another freshman. He shuffled up to the sink, still a little queasy. The nob squeaked as he turned it on, sending water splashing into the sink. He cupped his hands and wet his face. He stared into his reflection, taking notice of his blond hair sticking out past his ears and the short, soft, sandy mustache that was *almost* starting to look less awkward and more manly. He watched his eyes flick to the side, observing the horseplay going on behind him.

Mac was leading the pack, as usual. Instigating almost every conflict that took place in the locker room.

"You're not part of *my* family until you earn it, *Fresh*."

"Yeah, you have to earn it!" Tubby, Mac's *right-hand-man* chimed in.

The smallest of the three, Petey, who was always playing catch up to their shenanigans added his two cents.

"To be on *this* team, you have to prooove that you're family."

"Yeah, so how about you prove it by taking a bite out of that urinal cake,"

Mac challenged.

The scrawny freshman, too short for his big shorts, tried to laugh it off as if they were joking. But Mac, wearing his cut-off "300 Club" powerlifting t-shirt, grabbed him, picked him up like a loaf of bread, and shoved his face down into the dirty urinal.

"We're not kidding, Fresh! Eat it!"

Tyler stared at them in the mirror, wrestling over his own thoughts of right vs. wrong. He shook his head, took a deep breath, and flicked the water from his hands.

His voice started softer than he wanted and ended louder than he anticipated.

"Guys, c'mon. You heard Coach. We're a family, and families don't treat each other like that."

Tyler turned around and dried his hands on his shirt. He studied them, half smiling half clenching his jaw, waiting for each one to slap each other on the back, laugh it off, and walk away.

But they didn't. Tyler's words fell short of their shenanigans.

Instead, Mac pushed the tiny freshman's nose down until it was nearly touching the pink urinal cake.

The poor freshman struggled to breathe above the stench of urine and spit.

"Dude, c'mon! I'm not going to eat it. That's disgusting! Let me up!" He had ahold of each side of the urinal, pushing, fighting to keep his face from plunging further into the dirty urine and dip filled bowl.

The other linemen cheered on their buddy.

"Eat it! Eat it! Eat it!"

Tyler scowled and grit his teeth. He balled up his fists as he marched over to them. Mac looked up just as Tyler shoved him away from the urinal. The freshman caught his feet and tried to run. But he ran right into Tubby's gut and stopped him in his tracks with a bearhug.

Tyler held up his hands, pleading with them.

"Come on, brother. We're a family. Let's act like it."

Surprised by Tyler's intervention, Mac aimed his anger at him.

"Oh, like *your* family? You think we didn't hear about it? We know that you got your dad arrested. How pathetic, to snitch on your old man. *Family?* Get out of here with that bullshit."

Tubby laughed and backed up his buddy.

"And trust me, we know *allll about* your slutty sister, too!"

Tyler's eyes grew large with rage fueled further by the group laughing in his face.

With them all distracted for a moment, the freshman tried to pull away, again. But he was cut off at the door by Petey, who pushed him up against the wall, still chuckling and rattling like a bobblehead.

"Whoa. Whoa. Whoa. We didn't tell you to leave yet. Here you go, Mac."

Mac sneered at Tyler's red face and strutted over to the freshman, picked him up, pinned his swatting hands, and carried him like a sack of corn towards the urinal, again.

"Get back down there and eat it, shrimp."

Tubby's face lit up, and he grinned. He ripped down his pants and positioned his groin in front of the freshman's dangling head.

"No. No. Eat this instead," he laughed.

All three linemen laughed as Mac swung his head back and forth towards Tubby's naked waist.

Tyler squeezed his fists until his knuckles turned white.

"That's enough! Let him go!"

Mac continued to torment the freshmen, laughing at Tyler's strong stance beside him. But Tyler had enough of Mac's hazing. He cocked back his fist, right in front of Petey's wide-eyed face, and swung as hard as he could, pounding Mac in his dimpled chin. Mac stumbled back, letting loose of the freshman, who backed pedaled towards the door in shock. Mac's legs buckled as he lumbered backward, sending him to the ground with a loud grunt.

"I said that's enough!" Tyler's eyes were focused, fierce, and raging mad.

The linemen with his shorts down tried to yank them up quickly, but it wasn't fast enough. Tyler swung again and connected just below his eye, sending him sprawled out across the bathroom floor with his shorts hanging low around his waist, exposing his buttocks in a crumbled heap of muscle and testosterone.

Mac, was back on his feet rubbing his jaw.

"What the hell, man?! Are you mental, or something?"

Mac took an aggressive step towards Tyler. But Tyler was quicker than him. Tyler was more agile than him. Tyler stepped to the right and did a "swim move" that his receivers coach taught him to get off the line when the defense was in press coverage. Confused by his whiff and miss, Mac turned his head to see Tyler kick his cleats into his rear end, sending him headfirst into the wall.

Shaken and bloody, he stood up dazed and wobbly. Tyler headed towards the door and the freshman who was frozen in place.

"I... am **not** my father!" Tyler mumbled as he walked away.

The freshman's eyes darted back and forth from Tyler to the two linemen on the ground, to Petey who was in just as much shock as the freshman was. When Tyler got close enough to him, he relaxed and pat him on the back.

"Thanks. Thank you. You saved me, man. I mean... thanks for standing up for me."

Mac groaned to his feet, blood dripping down from a gash in his forehead.

"I'm not done with you boys yet!" Mac wiped the blood from his eyes, grunted and huffed as his slow, heavy steps came at them.

Tyler stepped in front of the freshman. "Look, man. It's done. It's over. Let it go." The freshman saw his moment to run and escaped through the door, yelling for Coach through the locker room.

But, by the time Coach and the freshman had made it back into the bathroom, there was blood splattered on the wall, the mirror and Tyler's hand, and there were three moaning linemen writhing in pain on the floor.

"What in the hell...?!" Coach thundered at the sight of his bloodied defensive linemen lying on the floor.

Tyler looked his coach in the eyes and wiped his bloodied hand across his football t-shirt.

"They had it comin', Coach."

"Yeah, they were trying to get me to eat a urinal cake, and his... his... pecker!" The out-of-breath freshman yelled.

"Is that right?" Coach boomed with his hands on his hips, evaluating the mess on the floor. "Get your asses up and get the hell out of here!" He thundered, pointing towards the door.

The three linemen groaned and huffed as they got to their feet and staggered out of the slamming door.

"Make sure you drink plenty of fluids for all the running you'll be doing tomorrow," Coach yelled towards them as they left the building.

Coach looked Tyler up and down.

"What the hell did you do to them?"

Tyler looked at the freshman and at the other coaches and players now gathering in the doorway.

"Nothin'. I just taught them a lesson about family."

•　•　•　•　•

"Mr. and Mrs. Handler, thank you for coming in on such short notice." Tyler's football coach had set up two padded folding chairs in front of his desk. Jim and Ashley sat across from his desk which was decorated with pictures and medals hanging from trophies. Centered in front of Coach was an open playbook. It was obvious that he had been busy erasing pencil marks and drawing fresh, new, directional lines, sending "X's" and "O's" to different spots on the white paper. Jim had earned Coach's curious stare when he nonchalantly readjusted the trophy in the corner of his desk to make it align more properly.

"We were very worried to hear that Tyler was involved in another "incident," Jim replied.

Coach shifted in his seat and folded his hands over the top of the playbook.

"Well, yes... yes, he was. But... I hate to say it, but this time, although I don't necessarily agree with striking another teammate, this time, I have to admit that I agree with what he did."

"What exactly did he do?" Ashley spoke up, her words slightly blurred together.

"Well, as I mentioned briefly on the phone, he got into a bit of a fight in the bathroom with some upperclassmen, defensive linemen. Go figure. And I'll tell you what, that kid has some fight in him... ehh, borderline anger issues, but fight, nonetheless. With that said, I know that there is one freshman who is *very thankful* that Tyler stepped up and stopped the hazing that was happening behind my back."

Jim reached over and gently placed his hand on Ashley's. Surprised, she flinched for a second, but quickly joined the show and affectionately rubbed his hand with her other.

"Tyler knows that we don't condone any kind of violence in the Handler house," Jim said matter-of-factly.

Ashley's brows scrunched before she could stop them. But she recovered with a soft smile.

"We try to teach respect and courtesy in our household." She affirmed.

Coach missed the little hints that danced around his office between the two of them. He fell for it, just as many others had when Jim and Ashley were in public. Their family was *perfect*, their love-life was *perfect*, their character *flawless*, their problems *nonexistent*... or, at least, that was the act that they were so used to playing. Putting on a "face" for the crowd had become so routine over the years that it felt more like a double life. Although, Ashley certainly admired the moments when they could pretend that it was like "the old days," back when their love was strong, and Jim's hands were soft.

Jim was a master manipulator. It came naturally to him, like an instinct or reflex. He was so filthy with subconscious guilt that his mind had convinced him that his own lies of stability and homeliness were real. Regardless of his intentions, there was still some resemblance of affection in his touch. Ashley yearned for that. She lived for that.

"Now, don't get me wrong, I think Tyler is a great kid who is discovering who he is, and I respect his hard work and dedication to the program. However, even if his reasons were justified, we can't have our players fighting one another. It's just too disruptive to the *family* attitude that we're trying to build here. Understand?"

Jim looked at Ashley, smiled and nodded.

"Yes sir, we certainly agree with you. Tyler will absolutely be reprimanded when we get back home."

"Look, I don't want to kick him off the team or anything, or even let this get out of 'the locker room.' I simply want him to understand that there are consequences for his actions, just as there are for *you*... or me... or any of us. We're all held accountable for our actions. Right?"

Jim squeezed Ashley's hand, let go, and patted her on the thigh.

"Absolutely. There are always consequences for the decisions that we make. Quite frankly, I... *we've*... been trying to get our children to understand that, lately. I think this will become a great teaching tool."

"I agree. Jim, you know, as a father myself, I just pray and hope that I do enough to teach them how to make the right decisions. You know, the ones that *we* should have made back then."

Coach laughed, and Jim and Ashley joined him.

"Again, just to be clear. I respect what Tyler did. Hell, I even appreciate it. He stood up to bullying, which we don't tolerate here, and I am thankful for his courage. But, we need to learn to deal with things in a less violent manner. I want to coach… I want to *teach* my kids how to control their anger, their emotions. I think that's important in life, being able to control the mechanisms that form our actions. Wouldn't you say?"

Jim arose, "Well…" Ashley and Coach followed his lead. Jim extended his hand and Coach shook it.

"I think you're doing a hell of a job, here, Coach. I agree with you one-hundred percent. And I'll… *weee,*" he smiled and rubbed Ashley's back, "will handle it on our end, at home. Thank you for letting us know. I appreciate it."

"No problem, Jim. Thank you both for coming in. I look forward to seeing you both involved in the program this year. Take care, now."

When Jim and Ashley returned home, the pizza delivery man wasn't far behind them. Hoping to surprise him, Ally had ordered her dad's favorite double Pepperoni and pineapple pizza.

After icing down a drink for himself, Jim took a seat in his favorite chair, while Ashley and Nikki set the table for dinner. Ashley had convinced Jim that a nice family sit-down-dinner *is exactly what this family needs*. Ally rushed down the stairs wearing one of his old XL flannel shirts, hopped onto his lap and wrapped her arms around his neck.

"I missed you, daddy. Did you miss me, too?" she asked in a high-pitched voice.

Jim shook her loose from his neck and grimaced.

"Not now, Ally. It's been a hell of a day. Don't you have something you could be doing?" He said more harshly than he intended.

Taken aback and disgusted, Ally pouted her way off his lap and stood defeated beside him.

"But I got you your favorite pizza, daddy." She sounded more wounded than anything.

"Yeah. Thanks." Jim took a sip from his old whiskey glass and unfolded the newspaper, flipping it quickly to the police reports.

Red-faced, Ally crossed her arms and stomped her foot.

"Why can't you just love me like you used to?!"

She stormed off through the living room walkway, grabbed her phone from the stand, and texted Brian that she was on her way over. She ripped his letterman jacket from the hook on the wall, ran out to her car, and spun gravel as she pulled out of the drive.

Tyler came down the steps in his usual cut-off shirt and athletic shorts to see what the commotion was about.

"What was that all about?" he asked.

"Just another one of her fits," Jim said without lowering the newspaper. "Pizza's in the kitchen, let's eat.

Jim tossed the newspaper on the stand, sighed heavy, groaned out of his chair, and followed Tyler into the kitchen. Ashley pulled out Jim's chair at the head of the table and put her hand on his shoulder as he sat down. She loved nights like these, where the family could all co-exist.

Ashley smiled, running her hands through the back of his hair. He shut his eyes for a moment and then quickly shook her away. Satisfied with her small victory, she dug into the box of pizza and put a slice on four of the five plates.

"Ally's not joining us?" She asked.

Jim shook his head.

"Nope."

"Well we can still try to have a nice dinner, can't we?" She said as she passed around soda and a plate of pizza to each seat. Nikki ripped off four sheets of paper towels, passed them around and sat down beside her mother.

"Pizza's cold." Jim was starting to feel the float of whiskey in his veins.

"Oh? I can heat it up for you?" Ashley offered.

"How about you do it, Nikki?" Jim held up his plate in her direction.

Nikki, mouth half full, stopped chewing.

"Mom just said she would." She mumbled, confused.

"I don't care what mom said, I'd like for you to warm it up for me."

The arrogance in his voice sent a shiver down the back of Nikki's neck. Tyler sensed the tension rising and his father's cocky undertones. He wanted to break his father's attention from his younger sister to him.

"So, what did Coach have to say? Am I still on the team?"

Ashley took a sip of her wine.

"Yes. But this whole... *situation* is something that we need to discuss."

Jim took a lengthy last drag from his whiskey glass and slammed it on the table, empty.

"I'm tired of you bringing unwanted attention to this family!" He roared, unexpectedly, taking everyone by surprise, and making Ashley jump, spilling her wine.

"Jim, let's calm down. We can discuss this after dinner." She said dapping at the small puddle of wine with her paper towel.

He stood up, nearly knocking over his chair as he noisily kicked it out of his way to refill his glass.

"I think we should talk about it now! Quite frankly, I don't think there's much to talk about. You're not going to bring unwanted or negative attention to this family! I don't need that right now!"

Tyler straightened in his chair. He could feel the heat building in the room. The refrigerator kicked on, humming in the pause of raised voices. Tyler's senses tuned into the stillness in the air. He could hear the slow and steady drip from the faucet. He watched as the water would build around the rim until it was too heavy and then let go, thumping a splatter down onto a dirty plate still in the sink from lunch.

His focus returned to his father's eyes. There was rage building inside of them, like the faucet, and Tyler could feel its weight about to fall.

"Yes sir, I understand. I just –"

Jim pounded the Jim Beam bottle onto the counter.

"Shut your mouth! I don't need your backtalk!"

"Jim! Calm down! Please!" Ashley pleaded with tears building in her eyes. She just wanted a nice, peaceful evening where the family could act as if they were still *a family*.

"Come on dad, come eat with us. I'll warm up your pizza." Nikki tried her best to act like she wasn't afraid.

"I will sweetheart, I will," Jim said leaning against the counter, his arms folded over his chest, his glass just below his chin, sipping in between sentences as if his whiskey was the fuel that kept his words flowing. "But, first, I want Tyler to understand me clearly. There will be no shame brought into this house by any of you."

He pointed his glass loosely in each of their general directions.

Tyler was becoming fed up with his father's pointing fingers. With his fists on the table, staring at the grease shining in small puddles in each Pepperoni, he felt his body begin to boil.

"Oh, I guess only *you* can do that?" He said nearly under his breath.

"What?! What did you just say to me, boy?!"

Jim finished his whiskey in a head back gulp and tossed his glass into the sink, shattering it onto the dirty plate.

Ashley stood up, tears now streaking her face, and immediately began cleaning up Jim's mess.

"Please, Jim. Go eat. Ally ordered your favorite pizza. Just enjoy it." Ashley's attempt to calm the beast fell short of its mark.

"Fuck Ally," Jim muttered, rolling up his sleeves.

Tyler stood up defiant with hate in his eyes and revenge on his breath. He was ready to protect his family.

"You already have, asshole!" he growled

In two long steps, Tyler lunged at his father, knocking him against the humming fridge, and to the ground. They wrestled for a few moments until Jim maneuvered his way on top.

"Stop it! Stop it right now!" Ashley cried.

She tried to pull Jim off of Tyler. But Jim forcefully shoved her back into the table, turning it and the pizza over onto the floor. Bawling, Ashley shifted to her knees as blood trickled from her nose.

Nikki cowered back against the wall covering her ears and squeezing her eyes shut. She tried counting slowly to ten, hoping that it would all disappear and be over with. But by the time she mumbled *ten* and opened her eyes, Jim and Tyler had ripped down all of her poems and Ally's drawing from the fridge. There was blood smeared on them now. The pots and pans left hanging around the stove were swinging, others were rocking on the tile.

"Dad, please!" She begged as the two of them twisted about on the kitchen floor.

Jim rolled Tyler to his back and smacked him across the face. Tyler tried to wiggle free but couldn't. Nikki knew that she had to try and distract her father. She knew that she had to help her brother.

"Dad! Dad! I love you! Please!" Nikki hurried over to them and hugged her father, kissing him several times on the cheek.

"Just take me! Take me!" She cried. "Take me upstairs with you. Please!"

She stroked the back of his head, running her fingers through his hair, sliding her hand along his neck, trying to calm him down, trying to ease his anger, giving everything that she had to pull his attention from Tyler.

Tyler, on his back, extended his arms out, grabbing Jim's throat, restraining his father from him. Nikki's intervention started to have its effect.

Jim's teeth unlocked, his jaw eased, his eyes widened, letting in more light. He relaxed. In that instant, staring into Tyler's bloody face, feeling his son's hand wrapped around his own throat, Jim could see the chaos he was causing, he felt the ravage in his chest, and for just a moment, he questioned it all.

"Get off!" Tyler grunted, shoving him up further away from his face.

Jim's eyes refocused, and he clenched Tyler's shirt collar, twisting it within his tight grasp. He pulled himself inches from Tyler's face.

"Don't you **ever** try that again! You hear me, boy?!" Jim growled.

Tyler grunted and groaned. The pain of the tackle and wrestling on the floor was starting to sink in. He realized that he was bleeding from his elbow, and it started to weaken, bend, give in under Jim's weight.

Jim pushed himself up with his left hand, cocking his right hand back behind his ear. There, he hovered, contemplating his next move. But Nikki reached out and grabbed his hand, held it softly, rubbed it for a moment and then tugged him towards the stairs, towards his bedroom.

Ashley was weeping on the floor, a puddle of blood dripping beside her. She looked around at the broken dishes, pizza, and mess all over the floor. She gazed at the scene before her, her children showing more fortitude than her, more valor on this battlefield than she could muster. She felt little, helpless. She felt unimportant, broken. She felt as though the world didn't need her anymore.

Jim shook Nikki's hand from his, clenched his fist tight and brought it down hard onto Tyler's left cheek. Tyler's hand fell from Jim's neck, and he moaned in defeat. His face instantly turned red and puffy. He rolled around on the floor holding it, wincing, cursing his father with silent words.

Jim stood up, made his way over to the spilled box of pizza, wiped his hand on Ashley's back, grabbed a slice, and took a bite.

He took in the mess that he made with pride. Then, he glanced seductively at Nikki and nodded towards the stairs.

"Alright, let's go."

He lumbered toward the living room, pizza in one hand and her tiny hand in the other. She looked back at Tyler still on the floor as he pulled her, dragging her to his den.

"Don't! Dad, don't you do it!" Tyler huffed from the kitchen floor.

Nearly to the stairs, Jim paused, looking back with a sense of accomplishment spreading over his face and grinned.

"I can do whatever the hell I want, son... and there's not a single damn thing you can do about it. I'm Jim Handler... I saved this town."

Then, he disappeared up into the stairway darkness, tugging his prey behind him.

NINE.
THE RESOLUTION

2018, September – 2018, October

Ally had stayed over with Brian again. It was becoming a consistent escape on days when her father wouldn't give her the attention that she wanted. She discovered that there was something very warm and familiar about falling asleep in Brian's strong arms. She was comfortable there with him stroking her hair, reminding her of how beautiful she was. Brian always gave her more attention and love than she could understand. She needed that, especially on the days that her father broke her heart.

As the sun peered through the gap between the curtains, bringing light to her young, pale face and waking her, she opened her eyes to meet Brian's rough face and smiled. He had been awake for the last few minutes watching her sleep, watching her steady breathing, in and out, up and down, so peaceful, so quiet, so much the opposite of how she had shown up to his house last night. She had him to thank for that.

Brian's soft words and reassurance calmed her to the core. When she was with him, she didn't even think about her father. Although, at times, Brian would pry when he knew something was wrong. Of course, she would tell him, or at least as much as she could before it all became too much. In those moments, he would hold her under his chin, stroke her hair, and let her know that he was there for her. That's all she needed. Just someone to make her feel alive. Someone to give her their undivided attention. Someone to make her feel important.

Now they both adjusted on their sides, facing each other, smiling. His smile lit her up inside, and hers made his cheeks tingle. They were two young kids in love, fighting through the pain and confusion of their high school years. She was his wounded puppy, and he was her rigid splint. They were meant for each other. They were put there in each other's lives for a reason. And, now, staring into his gentle, bright eyes, Ally knew what she wanted, what she needed... and climbing on top of him, she bent down to feel his lips and tongue on hers.

"I want you," he whispered.

"I need you," she whispered back.

He wrapped his arms around her, rolled her over onto her back, and wiggled between her legs. Then, brushing her hair away from her face, he leaned in to kiss her softly.

She pulled him tightly onto her mouth, wildly, aggressively, biting at his lip.

He pulled back, looking into her fierce eyes and smiled.

"Easy, Tiger. We have all morning."

He ran his fingers along her temple, tracing the back side of her ear and flipped her dark hair away from her shoulder. He moved in closer to her neck. She could feel the heat and tingle of his breath beneath her jaw. Gently, softly, lovingly he pressed his lips against her shoulder, kissing her along her clavicle, up her neck, and tickling her with his tongue just below her earlobe.

"You're so beautiful." He breathed into her ear.

She grabbed his face and yanked it into hers, jabbing her tongue into his mouth.

He slid his hand up her breast to the side of her neck. Lovingly and gently, he brushed his thumb back and forth, brushing against her earlobe, sending electricity and goosebumps tingling up the back of her head.

This drove her wild.

She squeezed his hips and pulls him into her hard. The bed squeaked back and forth with their movement.

"Faster! Brian, faster!" She demanded out of breath, digging her nails into his bare back causing him to flinch.

"Easy, babe," he laughed.

She gripped his hand firmly and guided it to her throat, tilting her head back and closing her eyes, she squeezed it tightly.

"Choke me. I want you to choke me," she moaned.

Brian hesitated, unsure if this is something that he was into or not. Deciding against it, instead, he slowed his rhythm and dragged his fingers through her messy, midnight hair.

"I love you, Ally," he said lost in her eyes.

With a deep breath, she yanked his hips into hers, hard and fast.

"Oh, God! Just like that!" she screamed pulling the pillow into her mouth and muffling her moans.

The bed knocked against the wall. Brian's notebook slid from his desk to the floor. He tried to slow down, to suppress the squeaking and banging. But she didn't care. She wanted the whole world to know that she was alive, that she could *feel*. She could feel the power of their movements, pulsing and thrusting, smacking and banging, she kept his pace fast and hard, rough and aggressive.

She jerked his hand up to her neck and squeezes.

"Choke me!"

He squeezed lightly, wanting to please her. But with her hand still on his, she clenched down forcing her air to be sucked in loudly.

"Like this," she forced out.

He held her neck firm in is hand. He could feel her pulse pounding at his thumb, the muscles flexing in her neck, making him feel powerful, in charge, dominant... *ashamed*. He could see her face turning red as she gasped for air.

He tried to let up, to let go.

"Harder!"

He wanted to make her happy. He wanted to satisfy her. He squeezed harder. She latched onto his back with her claws, thrusting her hips wildly.

"Oh God! Harder!"

He found her rhythm, hard and fast, hard and fast.

"Harder! Harder, **Daddy!**"

And, just as quickly, it was over with. Done. Finished off with two loud moans... and one confused, shocked young man.

They laid beside each other trying to catch their breath. Brian, staring at the ceiling, Ally looking out the window. He scrunched his face, sweat at his brow, trying to understand her deep desires. She, with a satisfied smile, was clueless about what her own lips had uttered.

A moment of breath and sweat went by.

"Babe," he said cautiously.

She rolled over and grabbed his hand.

"Yeah, babe? That was amazing."

"Well... I think... I think we need to talk about this."

"Talk about what? About how much I love you?" She grinned.

He squeezed her hand, let it go, and caressed her warm and damp cheek.

"Ally... that's not how you love someone. That's not *love*... that's... a sickness"

• • • •

That Saturday morning, as Ally pulled into her driveway from Brian's house, she had a lot on her mind. Brian's words "it's a sickness" crushed her, at first. She left upset, sad, angry, confused, and in tears.

Now sitting in the driveway, staring up at her big, white, country house, the black-shuttered windows on the second floor seemed like eyes staring down at her, *through* her. She felt judged. She felt betrayed. But most of all, she felt that he was right.

She sat there in her car listening to the morning birds chattering in the rising sun. Her thoughts consumed her, exhausted her. They made her chest tight and sore. She felt it deep down in the darkest halls of her existence that she had a sickness, that she was truly messed up. She knew that her abuse had created her condition. But for the first time in a very long time, she accepted that her father was a virus that was eating away at her health and her sanity.

With her head against the steering wheel, she started to sob. Buried in her thoughts, she just let go, crying loudly, violently, pounding her fists onto the dash, throwing her books against the windshield. She tore down the Polaroid of her on her father's lap just a few years ago for her thirteenth birthday and ripped it into pieces. She wanted to be rid of it. She wanted that memory gone. With a loud roar, she threw them out the window and watched as they scattered away on the breeze and out of her mind, like memories of her father's cold hands between her legs and her head between his. She cried and raged until the birds flew away until there was nothing left to give her company or comfort, except for those sad, black, heartbroken, second-floor-window-eyes which had watched it all come and go, the good, the bad, and the dirty. She glared at them for answers.

"Why? Whyyy?! Why me? Why us? What did we ever do so wrong?" she asked the black, paint-chipped windows and shutters fluttering against the wind.

But they said nothing. They *did* nothing. Just portals to the bright world outside and witnesses to the darkness inside. She wondered who had it worse, her or those old, shameful, dirty windows.

She took a few lasting, deep breaths. Wallowing in the misery was useless.

She sensed a need for action, a chance for restitution. But, for now, she cleaned herself up, pulled her messy, ebony hair back into a tight ponytail, and forged forward into the shadows of her home.

"What happened to you?" she asked after rounding the hallway at the top of the stairs and seeing Tyler all banged up.

"Nothin'."

He was shirtless at his desk, wearing nothing but his football shorts that Coach handed out during two-a-days and watching Dude Perfect videos on Youtube. His head was gingerly draped in his hand while he slurped down a Mountain Dew and iced a big red bump on his cheek with a frozen bag of peas.

"Nothing? It doesn't look like *nothing.*" You look like hell. But whatever. Did dad say when he'd be home? I really need to talk to him."

Tyler grunted. "Forget dad. I'd be ok if he didn't ever come home."

"Ohhh, so that's what happened." Ally leaned against the door frame, her attention perked. "What did he do this time?"

"Nothin'. I don't wanna talk about it."

"Come ooon. I'll hear about it from Nikki anyway."

Nikki, hearing the whole conversation from her room, looked up from her journal and shouted to Ally.

"It was crazy! Tyler tackled dad like he stole something! Then they got into a huge wrestling match! Dad was pretty much John Cena, clearly."

"Oh my God, seriously? Did you hurt him?"

Ally walked into his Ohio State football decorated room and sat on his Buckeyes bedspread, ready to hear the full story. Tyler paused Youtube and spun around to face her, still holding the bag of peas to his face.

"What kind of question is that?" Tyler mumbled through the bag of peas. "Does it look like I won?"

Nikki came rushing into Tyler's room and sat on the bed beside Ally, who looked at her as if she didn't belong there. Tyler shook his head at both of them.

"What is this, a party in my room?"

"Come on. Just tell me what happened."

Tyler tossed the peas on the floor and took a swig from his Mountain Dew.

"There's nothing to tell. After you left, dad was in a mood, got drunk, said some dumb shit, I stood up for you, aaand... *this* is what happened."

"Wait. You stood up for me? What do you mean? Was dad talking about me?"

Nikki tossed her blonde hair over her shoulder.

"Yeah, he didn't like your pizza."

Ally's disgusted face made Tyler laugh.

"Why are you so mean to her? She's your little sister. And last night, she pretty much saved my ass."

Tyler grimaced, picked up the peas, and put them on the back of his neck.

"You know, I don't understand why we can't just treat each other like we care? You know? Like we're there for each other. I mean, we're a family."

Ally crossed her arms in defense.

"What? Are you getting all soft and sentimental now? Did dad knock some screws loose, something?"

Tyler stiffened up and threw the peas towards the door. They bounced and crinkled against the bedroom trim.

"No, I'm serious. We've all been abused by that piece of trash, we're all in pain. I don't understand why we can't just be there for each other? You know?"

His comments made the room fall silent. Both of his sisters searched the floor for something to say.

"I care." Nikki's soft voice broke the silence.

"I know you do," said Tyler.

Ally bit her lip and looked up towards the corner of the room.

"I care too. It's just... I just miss when dad used to treat us like his kids, you know? Do you remember when he used to camp with us out in the yard? Well, until we heard too many *monsters* and came running in?"

They all chuckled, reminiscing of the days that didn't make them feel so ashamed.

"Or when he would take us fishing?" Nikki added.

"Or when he would toss the football with us," sighed Tyler.

They sat for a few moments in the quiet reflection of those "good days" of their youth.

Tyler forced out a loud huff of frustration.

"Look, dad completely messed us up. That's just the damn truth. We knew that well before therapy with Mike. And I'm sure we'll be messed up for a long time after, too. But… all I'm saying is… we have each other, right? We're brother and sister. We've been fighting the same fight and didn't even realize it. Hell, in my eyes, we're warriors."

He picked up his football from his desk and spun it into the air.

"And, if you ask me, I think it's time that we start acting like it."

. . . . . .

Today was the day. Today they would put their "plan" into motion. Today they would end their suffering with self-inflicted justice. Today they would end their father.

Nikki sat at her desk thumbing through her journal and rereading her poems about her abuse. She had already read, "At Daddy's Hands," four times in the last twenty minutes. Her lips moved along as she read it yet, again.

Resting her blonde tangles in her hand and tapping her pen on her opened journal, she thought about the last few weeks. She thought about all the events and suffering which had brought them all to this day, to this decision, to this defining moment of their childhood, and perhaps the most distinguished act of courage of their entire lives.

She chuckled out loud to herself about Tyler's commitment to leading them all to justice.

"If the system isn't going to do what's right, then we will," he started his speech, like some politician campaigning for re-election. "And if justice is going to be served, then let it be at the hands of his victims." He finished, nearly a week ago, standing in front of them, pacing back and forth, pumping his fist with emotion.

Our captain, our general, our fearless leader. Nikki remembered thinking as Tyler unfolded his plan to get rid of their abuser, their father, for good.

Nikki shut her journal and lingered at the family picture on the front of it that she had drawn with colored pencils the day her mom had given it to her. *It's just one of my old notebooks that I failed to fill*, Ashley had said, as if it wasn't as memorable as Nikki made it out to be. Nikki admitted that she wasn't as great of an artist as Ally when she finally showed Tyler the picture. In it was just the four of them: Ally in purple, Ashley in yellow, Tyler in black, and Nikki in green, all fishing at the pond behind their house. The light brown grass was slapped around the dark blue pond. A fish was dangling from their fishing poles while each of them were smiling broad and showing their teeth. Jim was nowhere to be seen. But behind them, tucked away, hiding in the grass, she had drawn a small dark snake with a bright red tongue.

At the time, Tyler had asked her if that was the snake that she had killed a few years ago, back when Ally nearly stepped on it while walking down the path to the pond, cluelessly paying attention to nothing but her phone. "Clueless Ally" had no idea that there was a copperhead snake just below her ankle.

"Snaaake!" Nikki had yelled, instinctively swinging her fold-up lawn chair wildly at its head. To the surprise of them all, it was a direct hit which left the snake twisting and rolling for nearly five minutes as they watched, *eww-ing* and *aww-ing*, until it had eventually stopped moving.

When Tyler had asked her about the snake, she gave it some thought and simply nodded her head, though, she knew exactly what and who her snake represented.

But now she thought of how closely that snake had come to striking and killing any one of them. How lucky they were, she thought, that she was blindly bold enough to work up a small step forward, let alone lash out and battle that predator to the death. She smiled and shook her head at the thought of comparing *that* moment to *this one*. She hoped that she could muster the same courage and fearlessness as she instinctually did that day.

Tyler knocked lightly on her door causing her to jump and kick the leg of her desk.

"Ouch! What the heck?! What are you doing, creeper?" She asked rubbing her foot and trying not to laugh along with Tyler.

"That was great. It seems like you're all ready for our mission tonight. Let's just hope that nobody makes a small knocking sound, or you'll be done." Tyler teased her.

"Shut up." She tried to laugh, but the reality of the situation set in, and seeing it on his sister's face, Tyler walked over and hugged her.

"I'm sorry. Look, everything will be fine. It'll be alright. We went over the plan, like, a million times. You got this. *We* got this!" He rubbed her back while she rubbed her big toe.

Ally, hearing the noise from Nikki's room, came to see what the drama was.

"What are you two douches doing?" She asked laying across Nikki's

Wonder Woman bedspread.

"Douches? Classy." Tyler shook his head, a small grin played at his eyes. "How about you? Are you ready for tonight?"

Ally looked down at the bedspread and picked at a loose thread hanging near the heart of Wonder Woman herself. She cracked her neck from side to side and then massaged it out of habit.

"I think so. I guess I sort of have to be, right?"

Just then, Ashley came walking through the hall with the laundry basket. She knocked on the open door and smiled to see them all in one room together. She wiped her messy blonde hair from her lips with her arm.

"Dirty laundry?" She nudged the basket pressed onto her hip in their direction.

"Already threw it in," Nikki said, "thanks."

"How about you two? Now or never. I'm throwing it in right now." She cocked her head and gave them the eye that she gave when she said something that they should do, but still gave them the freedom to make their own decision.

"Nah, I'm good."

"Me too." Ally smiled, hoping that her mother didn't ask what they were all talking about.

"Ok, then." Ashley turned to walk away and then paused. She spun back around with a serious but warming look on her face.

"You know, I've noticed that you all have been spending a lot of time together these last few weeks...."

Oh, no! She knows! Ally thought instantly.

"I just want to tell you all how much that warms my heart. I love you guys. Even if I'm horrible at showing it. You know that, right? That I love you with all my heart?" She smiled a warm, contagious smile that Tyler hadn't seen her use in quite some time.

"We know, Mom," Nikki started, "and we love you too... especially when you do our laundry." She giggled.

They all laughed together, shifting eyes back and forth during the awkward pause afterward.

Ashley stood in the door admiring her beloved children. She realized that she hadn't done that nearly enough recently. Now with the weight of a heaping basket full of dirty clothes and puffing at the wild hair tickling her face, she took it all in. The whole scene, her three children, who seem older than she remembered them, the smell of Tyler's sweaty clothes, of Nikki's *overused* perfume, and Ally's jet-black hair, straightened and combed, playing at her freckled cheeks. Ashley wanted so badly to reach out and kiss those cheeks, to pull each of her kids into her heart, to feel them, to hug them, to love them, and keep them all *right here, right now* in this moment, before they were all too grown to hug and kiss their mother.

Shaking her love-lit face, Ashley winked and headed out the door and down the stairs to the laundry room.

They listened as she lifted the lid while singing softly to herself, started the washer, and did her motherly tasks to show how much she loved them, how much she still wanted to take care of them. She was completely oblivious to their planned conclusion for this self-liberating evening.

"That was... uh, weird." Ally raised her brows at Tyler, who shrugged.

"Must be having a good day."

• • • • •

Jim was sipping on his third Jim Beam and Coke, which Ally had poured for him. It was a little on the heavy side, but he didn't seem to mind. He was watching NCIS in *his* chair while Ashley cleaned up the dishes in the kitchen. It had been a calm and quiet few days. There had been no fighting, no arguing, no apparent evil lurking around in the shadows. For now, the Devil was at bay and Ally wanted to call it off, suggesting that maybe he had changed. On those rare decent days, she clung tightly to hope. But Nikki and Tyler convinced her that it was time to face their demons. It was time to take back their lives.

"Dad," Nikki said, stepping through the walkway into the living room, "I'm... I'm ready for our *talk*."

"What? Oh, yeah." Jim looked at his shiny silver watch. It was just after 8 p.m., "I guess it is getting a little late." He ran his hand along his thigh and back up again to his crotch, adjusting himself. "Yeah, we should probably do it before it gets much later." He downed the last of his Jim Beam and groaned out of his love seat recliner. "Let's go." Was all he said as he passed her and headed up the steps.

Ashley watched from over her shoulder as he led Nikki up to their bedroom. She hadn't taken any pills today and had simply enjoyed one glass of wine for dinner. She was aware of Nikki's fate but didn't know how to stop it. Jim had beat her bloody the last time she had confronted him about what was happening to her children. So, she just watched with disgust, with sadness, and with weakness, as that son of a bitch led her daughter by the hand, up the steps, and into the bed that they still shared.

Nikki gave Tyler and Ally a quick look as she passed by their opened and waiting bedroom doors. They were pretending to watch TV, anxiously waiting for them to walk by. As soon as they did, Tyler looked at Ally, held up two fingers and mouthed "two minutes" across the hall. She let out a heavy sigh and closed her eyes. She was still holding onto something, still battling right and wrong. Deep down inside of her, she still wanted her father back. But, she could see the death inside of Nikki's eyes, and despite their differences, she had an aching to protect her younger sister.

Jim shut the door and turned on the nightstand light.

"So, how's school going?" He asked nonchalantly as he took off his shirt. This cycle of abuse had become so normal to him now that he was comfortable enough to engage in small talk. Of course, it wasn't always that way. The first several times Nikki kicked and punched. But she surrendered after he squeezed her throat and threatened to pull the life right out of her.

Nikki stood there watching her father undress down to his boxer briefs, stalling, hoping that her brother and sister would rescue her soon.

"It was okay. How was your day?" She hoped conversation would stall his intentions.

Jim chuckled, almost as evil, almost as empty as the act that he was so eager to commit.

"Fine, I guess. Now, come over here. Sit down." He lowered himself to the bed and pat the comforter beside him.

Nikki walked gently, still stalling, still burning the seconds away.

"Come on, I don't have all night. Take off your shirt." His words were slightly slurred.

Nikki slid off her shirt, leaving on her bra, and sat on the bed beside her father.

He ran his hand along her shoulder, then her neck.

"You're starting to grow up, you know," he said casually. "Soon, you'll be a woman. Soon, I won't have much use for you." His words seemed more like thoughts spoken out loud than conversation.

She ignored him, sitting on the bed shirtless as her father ran his hand over her body. She closed her eyes and tried to take herself away from his rough hands and whiskey breath. Her breathing became deep and controlled. She focused on her chest moving in and out, on her shoulders rising and falling. In her mind, she counted after each breath, watched as the numbers faded into existence in her head. She felt them. She created them. She became them.

It was one of the few precious things that she had learned from her father before he set out to ravish her. It was a generous gift he gave her, the day that she had walked in on Ally cutting her forearms. She had nightmares for days after seeing her sister's blood. One night, after waking up the entire house after screaming herself awake, Jim gently explained to her his secret about how he would calm himself after nightmares when he was a kid. He leaned down close to her ear and whispered: "just close your eyes, think of somewhere happy and safe, breathe in slow and deep, count slowly to ten, and back down again – if you have to." It was a technique that she had mastered by now.

"I wonder what I'll do once you're a little older." He was definitely thinking out loud now. "I suppose I'll just have to find someone else to love as much as you."

His words pierced her concentration, and she cringed at the thought of someone else facing this torture. She sucked in air loudly through her nose, tried to find her strength, and started counting again.

He stood up and slid off his underwear.

"Go ahead." He motioned, standing in front of her.

Ally was on her way back up the stairs with another strong drink for her father. Tyler was searching through his sock drawer for the bottle of Percocet he swiped from his mother's purse last night.

Ally rounded the corner into Tyler's room.

"Hurry," he said, "she can't stall forever."

He ripped open the pills and poured them all into the Jim Beam. Ally swirled the drink with her finger, letting them dissolve.

"C'mon... c'mon." Tyler encouraged until they fizzled out and blended with the amber drink. Tyler looked at Ally and nodded.

"Ready? Let's do this." Tyler handed her the glass. "Remember. Act normal."

She started down the hallway, careful not to spill any of the poison. Tyler was right behind her holding onto her shoulder for comfort.

She knocked on her father's door.

Jim was pulling his daughter's pants to the ground.

"Not now!" he shouted from the other side.

"I brought you another drink." Ally offered innocently.

Jim yanked off Nikki's pants and tossed them into the corner.

"Just leave it!" He yelled back, his words obviously slurring.

"Okay." Ally set the glass in front of the door, splashing some over the rim and onto the hardwood floor. *Crap.* She thought, wiping at it with her bare hand.

Then, they both hurried carefully back to Tyler's room. Wide-eyed, they stared at each other for a moment, and then peered around the door frame, waiting for their father to consume his fate.

Jim opened the door bare naked.

Ally and Tyler jumped back into the room, tripping over each other and bumping into the dresser, knocking over some of Tyler's football trophies.

Jim didn't notice. He was too focused on his drink, on his pleasure.

"Shh." Ally held her finger up to her lips.

Tyler set the trophies back onto the dresser, quietly. Ally crawled up to the door, barely poking her compact mirror out just far enough to see what was happening.

Jim stood in the black mass pouring out from behind him into the hallway light. He glanced around, grunted, and bent down to grab his drink. He stumbled, caught himself, rebalanced and reached down, again. This time he steadied himself on the wall. He wrapped his fingers around it firmly, felt its cold dampness, smelled the sweetness of alcohol and a splash of Coke as he pulled it up to his lips. The ice clinked against the glass. He stood there in the doorway – darkness behind him, light in front. He took a slow sweet swallow and turned and headed back into the shadows.

"Jim! Jim you bastard! You God damned bastard!"

Ally and Tyler snapped their heads toward each other and froze, eyes wide with shock, with fear.

Jim's shoulder slouched. He turned around annoyed, letting his drink dangle to his side.

His wife stood firm at the top of the stairs, like that old oak in the yard that outlasted last year's windstorm. Her arms were extended, Jim's duty pistol squeezed into her hands, her finger shaking on the trigger.

"I won't let you hurt us anymore! You hear me? You're done! You're through!" Her eyes narrowed as she pointed the pistol at Jim's thumping heart. "Now go to Hell!"

Shocked and startled to be staring down the barrel of his own Glock, he let the Jim Beam slip from his hand. It fell, wet and loud, splashing and shattering across the hardwood floor.

The loud crash and flash of glass caused Ashley to flinch. She yanked the trigger.

One shot ripped through the door frame. Wood splintered at Jim's cheek as he threw his hands up to cover his face. But there wasn't a second shot to follow the miss. Instead, there was the shrieking sound of terror and growl of frustration as Ashley realized the gun had jammed.

Jim saw his chance. He rushed her, spear tackling her across the hallway floor. The gun went skidding towards Jim's open door. Quickly, he was on top of her, pinning her with his left hand, and delivering blow after blow with his right. His knuckles cracking and smacking her flesh. Ashley's head whipped back and forth with each strike to her face.

Tyler jumped into action. He lowered his shoulder and threw himself at Jim, knocking him off of Ashley. The two wrestled around on the floor, each on top of the other for a moment, like two dogs in a backyard scrap.

But, Jim's drunkenness was a clear and obvious weakness. Tyler found himself on top and ripped a right hand across Jim's jaw. His nose gushed with blood, dripping across his lips. But this only enraged him. Jim went mad, swinging violently, like a maniac, striking Tyler multiple times in the face, shoulder, torso, and throat. Tyler rolled to the floor, but Jim didn't let up, his anger fueling his fists.

By the time Ally had gotten to them, Tyler was done. If she would have just moved a little sooner, a little quicker, perhaps, the two of them, together, would have stood a chance. But, alone, they were weak, they were fragile. Alone, they were victims. Jim saw her advance out of the corner of his eye and simply tossed her aside like an empty beer can. She smashed into the wall, hitting her head against the window sill, and knocking her unconscious.

Jim stood up and looked over his wounded enemy. Tyler was groaning in pain, covering his face, rocking side to side on his back and kicking against the hallway wall in agony. Ally was in a limp heap to the side of him. Even in that moment, he couldn't help but notice the top of her bra and cleavage hanging from her shirt. His stare lingered for a moment until he puffed away the images of her naked body.

He wiped his mouth clean and reminisced about how he used to choke her in bed while quickly taking his pleasure from her pain. He grunted and smiled at his accomplishments. But, the loud, furious barking of Shooter outside pulled him from his smile. His drunken imagination flashed back to the time that he had raged on like this before, years ago, flailing his anger at Ashley's face, only to have Shooter rip deep into his flesh. He took a quick look to his room to make sure that Tyler's bristly beast was not roaring out from the darkness to rip into him once again.

Ashley, bloodied and crying out in rage, barreled onto Jim's back. He stumbled to a knee, barely feeling her tiny fists on the back of his head. Then, like an annoying mosquito at a backyard party, he swatted her off and onto the floor.

Without thinking about it, without caring, and before she could fully get to her feet, Jim cocked his leg to the rear and brought it forward with all of his might, booting her just under the chin. She faded to black and motionless. Empowered by his strength, and enraged by his family's disobedience, he took it all out on her. One after another, he slammed his bare foot, his flesh, and bone against her limp body.

Blood splattered against the white walls, covering her face, and his foot. There was blood all through the hallway, smeared on the floor, and splashed across the family pictures hanging on the wall. There was blood on everyone's face, on everyone's hands, everyone's except for Nikki's.

She was frozen in horror, still in her bra and panties, standing in the doorway to her father's den, her hell. She was in shock, eyes gaping, hands covering her terrified and quiet shrieks. Shaking, she watched as her family devoured each other.

But it was the limpness of Ally's body that brought her out of that daze. The blood descending the side of her quiet face, her mouth open and gashed, and her nearly exposed breast from the awkward position in which she fell to her back, were pins jabbing at Nikki's heart. The sickness of seeing her sister so vulnerable, so exposed and lifeless, switched a wire inside of her that sparked a fresh, electric revolution zinging through her body and jolted her from her frozen state of shock.

With new adrenaline pumping her thoughts, she looked around frantically for an answer. She saw the black gun a few feet in front of her. Without thinking, she bent down and picked it up. It was cold, so cold in her little hands. Instantly, the weight reminded her of when her dad used to take her shooting when she was younger. *I know you're afraid, but you need to learn how to do this. Because, as you get older, you will need to take responsibility for your own safety... and whether you like it, or not, you may have to take someone's life to save your own.* He taught her how to line up the sights on her target, how to control her breathing and relax, and how to feel and squeeze the smooth round trigger instead of jerking it like her fishing pole.

But, most important at this moment, her father had taught her how to clear a jammed pistol.

She grasped the top slide with her left hand just in front of the sights. Gripping the checkered plastic handle of the weapon tightly, she yanked violently, pulling it to the rear. The jammed brass casing came loose from the chamber and fell with a sharp echoing *tink* onto the hardwood floor. She let go of the slide, sweeping a fresh, new, shiny, brass cartridge into the chamber. Raising the cold, dark, heavy tool to eye level, her hands shook as she aimed in on her father's chest.

Jim was still repeatedly booting Ashley in the face like a madman. He wasn't stopping. He had lost all control. His demons were in charge now. Jim was a hollow, empty man, filled with hate and rage from years of his own childhood abuse. He had bottled it all up inside and buried it deep down, hoping to never let it rise to his mind, again. It was that abuse, that tragedy, that evil atrocity that created the monster that Jim was today. It bred damning hate inside of Jim. So much hate. So much rage. So long without seeking help. It was too late for him. He had given up on salvation. He had given up on himself, on his family, on the system, on the world, on his life.

"Stop!" Nikki yelled. But Jim was too focused on his fury.

"Stop, Dad! Stop it! You're going to kill her!" She shouted over the top of the gun sights trembling at Jim's back.

Jim hardly even noticed his youngest daughter's high-pitched voice echoing above the thuds of his foot against Ashley's jaw.

Nikki had no choice. She knew that. She knew what she had to do. She knew that she had to shoot her father.

Time had slowed to a lifetime played out in the span every ticking second.

It all flashed before her; all of her sexual assaults burst into her mind at once, like a movie playing silently, a twisted horror flick, a gross fetish porno, a sick and vulgar, detailed film praising sexual abuse. It piled onto her heart like a load of dead bodies. She felt disgusting. She felt rotten. She felt wicked.

"I said STOP!" she yelled one last time.

Nothing. No one even knew she existed at this very moment. No one cared. No one paid her any attention. Everyone was beaten, finished, faded to black... end screen, film over, done, and gone. And anyone still alive in that moment, anyone able to hear her cries, were too focused on themselves. Their pain. Their wounds. Their hate. Their emotional carnage.

Nikki wanted to save them all. She wanted the hurt to stop. She wanted to free them from his spear.

Her finger tightened on the trigger. It was rigid and crisp. She held the sights on her father's twisting torso. He wouldn't stop. He would NEVER stop. She decided that she was going to stop him.

"Dad! Dad!"

Exhausted and slowed, he heard her faint cries over the demons in his head.

He turned to see her aiming at his chest, at his heart. His eyes narrowed. His fists clenched. His jaw squeezed. His naked, blood-soaked body lunged for her.

"Stop!"

A shot roared through the hallway, louder than any noise she had ever heard before. A thundering boom that shook the entire house. The window rattled, sending a streaking crack up into the corner. Picture frames, barely hanging on, fell from the wall and shattered.

Then, for a moment, everything was silent. Everything was dead. Then came the sounds of the wounded murmuring through the hall.

The shot pulled Tyler and Ally from their solitude. Each looked up, hoping for the rapture, wishing it was all over, begging to God.

But it was not God that they saw standing there in the doorway to Hell.

No, it was not God. It was their baby sister. It was Nikki. And she was holding a smoking gun.

Jim crumbled to his knees, grabbing and clawing at his chest. Wide-eyed and mouth gaping, it took him a moment to understand what had just happened. Then, there was a burning sting hammering at his chest.

With warm scarlet splattering from his mouth, he cried out.

"No! No, God! No!"

And, right there, in the hallway, beside his bleeding family, he collapsed, convulsed, and died.

Nikki felt sick to her stomach. Instantly she was ill.

She hunched over, leaning against the wall, and let it go. She let it **all** go. Everything bad that had ever happened to her came pouring out. Heave after heave, she threw up the sickness inside of her.

She spat and wiped her mouth clean with her arm. She arose from her knees to her feet and felt new. She felt reborn, more alive than she had ever been. She felt the torment let go of her heart. It smoldered up from inside of her. Like the gun smoke twisting towards the ceiling, her pain fluttered up through her chest, into her jaw, her ringing ears, her temples, and tingled out the top of her head, until she felt weightless and free.

She dropped the gun and looked down at her trembling hands. They were wet with perspiration, glistening in the sunlight refracting through the splintered crack of the hallway window. She extended her fingers, felt them grow and stretch to their full potential. They felt full, so full of life.

In her mind, she had no idea what her little hands could do. Now, staring at them, admiring each detail like a finely crafted tool, she squeezed them shut, tightly, with all of her strength, shaking with the pressure, with the force of her might.

She closed her eyes, sucked in deeply through her nose, and counted slowly to ten.

Then, she opened her hands carefully, peacefully, and watched in awe as the warmth, the color, the love rushed back in.

TEN.
THE HEALING

Five years later
2023, July

Tyler swatted away the smoke rising from the open grill on Ally's back patio. He poked at the sizzling ribeye steaks, rolled the black-lined hotdogs, and flipped the juicy burgers. He closed the lid, set his tongs on the hook, and took a swig from his red, white, and blue Budweiser can.

"Five minutes on the meat!" He yelled back to his mother, who had just carried out a big bowl of salad and set if on the American Flag themed tablecloth.

"You're doing great! Thank you!" She yelled back and rushed inside to get the covered dishes.

It had been five years since the day they liberated themselves from Jim. It had been five years of therapy, healing, recovery, growing, loving, and learning how to live as a survivor. It had been a difficult five years.

But, today, they were celebrating America's freedom with a backyard cookout at Ally's house, which was just a short drive down the road from where they all grew up. Her large open yard had a row of apple trees in the front and a raspberry patch along the wood line to the rear. There was a large oak tree with a tire swing outside her bedroom window on the side of the house, where the yard was littered with toddler toys. Not far from the tree was a red and yellow plastic slide and swing set. Beside it was a small pool with orange floaties thrown off to the ground in the front. The two-story cottage was quaint, but perfect for her, Brian, and their three-year-old daughter, Jessa Marie.

Ally's favorite part of her home was the back patio that Brian and Tyler had built just after Jessa was born. It overlooked a small creek and frog pond that gathered just below the wooded hills and valleys of Jackson Township. Most nights, after Jessa was put to bed, Brian and Ally would sit out in the flower-scented air on their hanging wooden swing, drilled into the angled half roof, and listen to the chirping tree frogs "talking" to the croaking bullfrogs in the pond. The trickling of the creek relaxed her and reminded her of the pond of her youth that she would spend hours playing around.

Today, the patio was decorated in small American flags, tiki torches, lawn chairs, and a large table full of food.

Nikki and Jessa Marie were chasing each other around the yard blowing bubbles at each other. Shooter, loose and free, would chase them excitedly, barking playfully and wagging his tail, before retreating to the shade of the oak for a quick, tongue-hanging breather.

Tyler manned the grill, while his girlfriend from Ohio University helped Ashley cut up vegetables on the speckled marble countertop in the kitchen. Brian threw more seasoning on the rotisserie chickens which were rolling over the top of glowing red coals and drifting smoke in the light breeze down by the wood line. His "Born 1776" shirt was damp with sweat, and he rehydrated with a cold Bud Light wrapped in an Ohio State koozie. Ally set the table with paper plates, plastic forks, and firework themed napkins. A few of their close friends mingled under the oak tree in the shade watching cornhole bags hit and slide up Brian's Ohio State cornhole boards. Mike and Mrs. V. tried to help set the table, but Ally shooed them away. They were now enjoying a cold drink over by Tyler, watching him master the grill, a skill he learned while away at college.

"How's school?" Mike asked, taking a sip of his sweet tea.

Tyler took a swallow of his beer, nodding his head before he answered.

"Going well, actually. I think I have a good chance of starting at receiver this year. Coach expects us to be in a bowl game, you know how coaches are… but, honestly, I think we have a shot."

"I tell you what, if you end up in a bowl game, I'll come and personally cheer you on, face painted and all." Mike chuckled.

"Hell, I'd like to see that." Tyler laughed. "You know, Mike, you can come down anytime and watch us play. I can probably set back a couple of extra tickets for you and your wife."

Mike slapped Tyler on the back and shook his hand.

"I'm going to hold you to that," he smiled, "don't you forget. Now, what's this I hear about you leading a sexual abuse survivors group on campus?"

Tyler flipped the burgers one more time and savored his sweating drink.

"Yeah," he said, nodding his head slowly, "I took the initiative to start a group. I wanted people like *us* to know that they're not alone, you know, to know that the pain fades away. I guess I just wanted to do my part. I wanted to help people who have had similar experiences as us... and we have. Mike, I tell you what, I hear it all the time, that group is making a difference in people's lives. I couldn't be more proud of that group of people coming together and supporting each other. It's completely inspiring."

Mike smiled big, and Tyler could tell by the light in his eyes that he was proud.

"Wow! Tyler, that's amazing! I truly mean that. You're an inspiration."

"Well, I doubt I could be as great as you," he grinned, "but honestly, I was thinking about declaring phychology or sociology as my major. I think I want to understand what makes people do these kinds of evil, disgusting things. You know, I just want to... I just want to try to understand it."

Mrs. V. rubbed his arm.

"You're a good kid. You know that? Your heart's in the right place. We're all so proud of you, Tyler... so proud of *all* of you." Mrs. V. gestured to his family. "I think you can do whatever you want in life. Seriously, I think you will be just fine."

"Thanks. I appreciate that."

Mike put his hand in his khaki pants pocket and motioned at Tyler with his drink.

"Well, I don't know how much it'll help, but I do have some old books that you could have. Maybe you can read a little bit this summer and see if it's what you want to do. I'll be honest, it's a lot of work, but the rewards of seeing people heal, of seeing how far they have come since they first walked in your door... that's beautiful. That's what makes it all worth it."

Mike started to get misty-eyed. He wiped at them under his glasses.

"Now, how are those steaks doing? I'm dying of starvation over here." He laughed.

Tyler lifted the lid and poked at them. "Looks done to me." He pulled all the meat from the grill and placed it onto a large platter.

Turning and walking carefully toward the table he sounded the dinner bell.

"Come and get it, you freedom loving American badasses! It's ready!" He shouted to the group.

"Tyler!" Ashley scolded as she set the last dish of pasta salad on the table.

"What? What I say?" He asked, smiling and placing the platter beside the mashed potatoes.

Ashley just smiled, even though she tried to tell them every day how much she truly loved them, she wasn't sure if her kids were aware of what they actually meant to her. She loved this time together. She had been clean of her addictions for the last four years. At first, she hated herself for all the time lost with her children. But, as they healed together, they had all grown so close to one another. Ashley thanked Mike, Mrs. V. and God every day for that.

Nikki, out of breath, carried Jessa Marie up to the table.

"Ewww, Tyler, those look burnt. You should have let a pro handle the grill," she teased.

"Well, that's ok, I'll just eat yours then," he jabbed back.

She laughed and placed Jessa Marie in her booster seat.

"Wellll, *okay*, now that you mention it, there might be *one* steak that isn't burnt. Dibs."

Ally and Brian brought the chickens over and placed them in the middle of the table. Ally stepped back and looked at all the food and people on her back patio.

"Wow," she said to Brian, "we're pretty lucky, aren't we?"

He grabbed her hand and kissed her on the forehead.

"Yes, we are, sweetheart. But everyone knows that I'm the luckiest. Just look how beautiful you are. Look at our beautiful child. I couldn't ask for anything else in this world."

He squeezed her hand and winked. Ally smiled back. Six years together and he still gave her goosebumps. He still loved her, despite her flaws, despite her past, despite her scars; He still loved her, and she thanked God every night.

"Nikki, you wanna say grace?" Ally asked.

"Sure. Let's hold hands."

Everyone circled the table and held each other's hands.

"Lord, thank you for this food that we're are about to eat, even if Tyler did burn it, please let it still taste good." She paused for the soft laughter. Her mother squeezed her hand, scolding her.

She continued. "Thank you for bringing us all together on this beautiful day to celebrate our freedom, and to give thanks for the blessings in our lives. Lord, we are absolutely blessed, and we thank you for your continued grace.

In Jesus' name, we pray, amen."

Ashley squeezed her hand again, but this time, it was to say, "I love you."

"Let's do this," Tyler said reaching for a plate.

"Wait!" Ashley threw her arm in front of Tyler. "I think we should go around the table and say what freedom means to us. What do you all think?"

"Aww, Mooom, c'mon!" Tyler groaned.

"I think that's a fantastic idea," Mrs. V. chimed in.

"Mom, seriously?" Ally protested.

"It'll be fun, come on," Ashley insisted. "I'll start.'

"Ok, fiiine," Tyler groaned.

Ashley looked around the table at her family and friends. She looked at the food, the beautiful yard full of toys, chairs, and happiness, and then at Ally's gorgeous house. She looked at the wooded hills and the birds circling above them. She looked at Ally, Nikki, and Tyler, and smiled.

"To me, *this* is freedom. Having the ability to stand here with you all, not high, not drunk, not bruised, or in fear. To laugh with you all, to eat, and share our stories. To me, freedom is as simple as loving your life. Which I most certainly do, now."

She dabbed at the tears building in her eyes with a napkin. Nikki, Ally, and Tyler all moved in to give their mother a group hug. They embraced each other, sobbing, squeezing each other tightly, loving each other more than they ever had. With a deep breath, they broke apart.

"Alrighty, then," Nikki said, wiping her face and laughing, slightly embarrassed. "Who else wants to make us cry, today? Mike? Mrs. V.? Brian? Anyone? I'm going to need another napkin."

They all smiled and laughed. All were warm with love under the summer sun.

Mike spoke up next.

"Freedom. What a big word." He bit his lip with thought. "Well, when I think of freedom, I think of all those abused and beaten kids who come to my residential facility. I think about how broken they are. How much hate they are filled with. And I watch them heal over the weeks, the months, the years. I watch them grow, and just like all of you, I watch them learn how to love again. Then, I watch them take that final walk out of the center's front door, turning around to smile and wave one last time," He squinted in thought, "and I think," his eyes shifted to the table, "no, I *know*... that *that* is what freedom is."

With his voice shaking at the end, he took a slow drink from his glass of tea. Mrs. V. rubbed his back and gave him a hug. His wife rubbed his hand and kissed his cheek. Everyone was smiling, everyone had goosebumps.

Mike lifted his glasses and squeezed the bridge of his nose, wiping away a couple of tears. "I nominate you, next," he grinned at Mrs. V.

"Oh, good gracious. How am I supposed to compete with you two?" She choked out over tears.

"Alright. Alright. Freedom. Well for, starters, freedom is our ability to live without fear and hate. Freedom from oppression, from racism, tyranny, slavery, corruption, and evil. But, personally, when I think of freedom, I think of my husband defending our freedoms. I think of the service men and women who volunteer to go to war, to fight to keep our nation free. I think of my students' faces, the ones who chose to enlist and serve their nation. I think of their sacrifices, them giving their lives or limbs, or mental stability so that I can live my life in peace and free will. When I think of freedom, I think of those sixth-grade faces that sat in my class making jokes and interruptions about sports, or girls, or each other... and I wonder if their mothers and fathers are as proud as I am to have had the opportunity to have had them in my life."

Everyone nodded their heads in agreement. Many were sniffling, some crying, and other's fighting to hold back tears.

"Well, freedom, to me," Tyler started, "is when I release from the line of scrimmage, and the defensive back whiffs while trying to get his hands on me, and away I go down the sideline for an easy touchdown. Yeah. Freedom."

He took a large gulp from his beer can and started to laugh along with the others. Ashley threw her fork at him, smiling, and the laughter erupted louder.

"Okay, okay. Freedom is... it's having a choice... the choice to do what you want to do, whenever you want to do it. I can go to class, or I can stay in and drink. I can play football, or I can join a chess club. I can date who I want, marry who I want, *be* who I want. I am free to choose what I want to choose. And for me, the best part about freedom is that I don't have to worry about messing up and making my father mad enough to beat me."

His comment hit Ashley hard, and she swallowed back the rage that Jim had left inside of her. Instead, she forced a smile, winked at Tyler, and mouthed "thank you" to him from across the table.

"Ally?" Tyler raised his brows grinning.

"Fiiine."

She adjusted her blouse, nervously.

"You all know that I'm not any good at this public speaking thing. So, I'm just warning you..."

She took a drink from her bottle of water.

"Ok. What does freedom mean to me? Well, besides what everyone else has already said, I think freedom stands for hope. I mean, having the ability to dream, to wish, to hope for something that you want, is freedom. Being able to chase your dreams, is freedom. I think that freedom is more about how we perceive things rather than what we are able to have. What I mean is... being free of mind. Free to let your mind wander without dangerous thoughts creeping in. Free to believe in hope without stressing over who will hate you for it. Freedom is a clear and open mind. One that does not want to harm itself. One that has confidence, love, and happiness. That's freedom... the ability to love others while still loving yourself."

Her eyes dropped, and she realized that she was rubbing her hand over the scars on her wrists and forearms. She sucked in a big breath of warm summer air. It smelled of seasoned food and honeysuckle. She shook her head, shaking away the thoughts of who she used to be, of a time when she wanted to hurt herself. But now it all seemed so distant, almost as though it wasn't even her. She felt new, reborn, loved. She felt alive, and she would do anything to keep it that way.

Ashley kissed her on the cheek and hugged her. Brian rubbed her back and squeezed her shoulder. He raised her hand to his lips and kissed it softly.

"I love you. I love you so much," he whispered.

"Not as much as I love you," she whispered back, rubbing his hand with her thumb.

She looked over at Nikki. "Nik? Wanna hit us with the good stuff? Maybe a poem about freedom, or maybe a passage from one of mom's new books?" She playfully pushed her "little" sister, who was now taller than her. "You and mom are so much alike, it's not even funny. How can one family have two amazing writers, thinkers, poets? And here, all I got were the looks." She laughed and stuck out her tongue.

Nikki stuck hers out, too, and threw a carrot at her big sister.

"Hey, now!" Ashley scorned. "Those are good carrots, don't waste them." She cocked her head and shook her finger at Nikki, then grinned.

"Okay, well... I'll hurry this along so we can eat Tyler's burnt burgers." She quipped one last time.

"Freeeedooom! You know, like Braveheart?" She laughed. "It's..." She shifted her weight, picked up her plastic knife, and ran her thumb along the serrations while she thought. "Freedom is being able to sleep peacefully, at night. It's sharing yourself with your family, completely, without secrets, without ill intent. It's being able to go into your sister's room and listen to her music, *without* her trying to push you down the stairs."

They all chuckled and looked at Ally, who was slightly embarrassed for the way she used to be overly dramatic and mean to her sister.

"But seriously, being free, in your own home, from pain, abuse, sexual assault... being free to play, or sing, or dance, without looking over your shoulder, without wondering when the next time your father was going to... assault you. That's freedom. Taking your life in your own hands, standing up to evil, to the wrong, and for the things that you believe in. That is freedom. Having the courage to say *No!* Having the courage to say *Enough!* Having the courage to fight back, to stand up for yourself, to know what is right and wrong. That's freedom."

She paused and looked around the table.

"Having the choice of who enters your body. **That's freedom.**"

• • • • • •

Tyler was throwing the football in the yard with Brian, while Ashley, Mike, and Mrs. V. helped clean up the patio. Most of their guests had gone home.

The sun was fading in the orange sky. In the distance, freedom lovers were already setting off *booms* from fireworks. The woods had just started to chirp, and the frogs in the pond were talking over each other. It was a beautiful summer evening, and the Handlers all felt it.

Nikki sat under the oak tree with Ally while Jessa Marie chased lighting bugs.

"You think you'll have any more kids?" Nikki asked.

"Umm, I don't know. If Brian has anything to do with it, *which I hope he does*, then we will have a million more," she laughed and winked at her sister who responded with an *"Ewww."*

Ally brushed her dark hair from her face and looked out toward the edge of the woods, toward the pond.

"But I think I'd like to just enjoy the three of us, for now. I don't know... maybe in a few years."

Nikki smiled and watched her older sister stare off into the orange sunset.

"But then they will be the same age difference as you and me. Do you *really* want them to go through the same sibling stuff that we did? I mean, you pretty much hated me for years, because I was way smarter than you. Obviously."

Nikki pushed Ally, and they giggled.

"Let's just hope that Jessa Marie isn't forced to listen to *Baby Questionmark's* poetry. They'll probably get along just fine, if not."

She picked a dandelion and threw it in Nikki's face. Nikki picked a handful of grass and threw it at Ally.

"Uh. Rude!"

They started to wrestle around on the ground giggling like they were little girls, again, but with different childhoods, happier childhoods. With three years of self-defense classes under her belt, encouraged by Brian, Ally was quick to pin Nikki on her back.

She straddled her, pinning Nikki's arms under her legs.

"Who's your favorite sister? Who's your favorite sister? Say it. Come on, say it."

Ally let her hanging dark hair tickle across Nikki's face.

"I'm not saying it! I won't do it!" Nikki shouted, trying to shake her head away from Ally's hair.

"Say it! Say, *Ally's my favorite sister!*"

"No! Never!"

Ally tickled and poked at her ribs until she twisted and giggled loudly.

"*Saaay, Ally's my favorite sister because she's prettier, smarter, stronger, and better at everything than me.*"

"I won't do it. I won't... I won't *lieee!*"

Ashley, Tyler, and Brian stopped to watch them both wrestle and play together.

"Better say it!" Tyler yelled cupping his mouth with one hand, holding the football with the other.

Nikki lifted her head and realized that they had an audience watching them and smiling. She couldn't let her sister win. She tried to twist and kick her way out from under Ally.

But, Ally had her locked down tight, and Nikki knew it. She growled in frustration, causing Shooter's ears to perk up, run over to them and soak Nikki's face with doggie-kisses.

"Okay! Okay! I give!"

Ally laughed and shooed Shooter away. He trotted over to his bowl of water and lapped it up. Ally's smug look frustrated Nikki.

"You gonna say it?" Ally smiled.

Nikki accepted that she had lost. Defeated, she went limp, rolled her eyes and grinned. Then, in her deep, annoyed, I-don't-care voice Nikki gave in, *"Ally's my favorite sister because she's prettier, smarter, and... fatter than me!"*

"Ugh! You little brat!" Ally started to tickle Nikki's ribs again.

"No! No! Stop! I give! I give!" Nikki rolled in laughter. "You're the best! The prettiest, smartest, strongest, better-at-everything-est sister in the whole wide world!"

Still, on top of her, Ally pressed for more.

"Annd?"

"Uhhh... aaand... you're not fat?" Nikki questioned.

Ally tickled her harder.

"You win! You win! And... I... *love you*! I love you! Come ooon, I love youuu!" Nikki was in full retreat, full red-faced laughter.

"Alright. Well, that's all you had to say. And I love you, too, you little shit."

Ally stood up and stuck her hand out to Nikki, who swatted it away.

"I didn't mean it! I had my fingers crossed!" Nikki teased.

"That's okay," Ally said helping her up and looking around, "I have *tons* of witnesses."

Jessa Marie stopped chasing fireflies and ran back over to Ally.

"Momma. Swing? Push me on the swing?" she asked with her arms extended.

Ally reached down, picked up her little dark-haired angel and gently placed her in the tire swing hanging from the oak branch.

Ally looked back at Nikki and grinned.

"Come help me push your niece."

Then, together, into a firefly-filled yard and a melting, orange evening, Ally and Nikki pushed sweet, smiling Jessa Marie back and forth into the thick, honeysuckle air. Tyler, Ashley, Mike, Brian, and Mrs. V., all with adoring smiles, watched on with enduring love as Jessa Marie reached her little hand out towards the light of a bright, burning bug and warm, glowing sky.

REAL STORIES FROM SURVIVORS

I reached out to my friends, fans, and local communities and asked if anyone would like to share their stories of abuse, advice for those who are being abused, or words about courage. I was amazed at the response I received. For many, they have been silenced by fear, shame, guilt, embarrassment, or hopelessness. I felt that they all deserved an opportunity to have a voice, a chance to be heard.

These are their stories. This is their voice.

When I was six, I was sexually molested and mentally abused by a teenage girl who lived next door. Her name was Melissa.

Melissa was an only child who lived with her mother and stepfather, and she had a long history of acting out, problems with authority, and was subject to screaming fits when she didn't get what she wanted. She was fourteen I think when I met her.

Melissa knew how to manipulate adults, gaining their confidence with platitudes and kindness. My mother never liked her, she always felt something was 'off' with the family.

It wasn't long before Melissa took my first French kiss by force, nearly asphyxiating me in the process. She then slapped me repeatedly and told me I was disgusting.

I was so shocked and bewildered, I had no idea what was happening. When I tried to get away, she pulled my long hair around her fist and yanked my head backward. She told me if I told anyone she would come after my little sister who hadn't even turned one yet.

"I know you don't lock your doors, I can walk right in in the middle of the night, and you will never see her again. Don't fuck with me."

She then demanded I come over tomorrow, or else. Terrified of what she might do to my sister I obeyed.

I did as she asked. That was the first time she fingered me, to my confusion, disgust, and shock— I orgasmed for the first time and immediately after I felt like I would be sent to Hell for it.

All I knew was that what she was doing was totally wrong— and I couldn't make my body stop liking it. It was mortifying, and I spent several hours strung out that day wondering what kind of monster I was for responding to what she did to me. I shouldn't have felt like that— it shouldn't have felt GOOD! I was traumatized by the craving to feel it again, hating myself, loathing her, and hating my body for what it was doing to me.

My mother finally had enough of Melissa's bad behavior and forbade is to be friends with her any longer, much to my relief. Her torture of me lasted for some months, but due to my youth and inexperience, I'm not sure of the timeline.

After Melissa and her family moved away, I had time to finally comprehend what had happened to me, and somehow even that young I knew it wasn't my fault at all. I carried the shame of it for a long time, the feeling of being tainted or broken like I wasn't ever going to be whole... but it didn't stick around.

I was blessed with a loving family who believed in Jesus, and through prayers and faith that God had so much good in store for me, I was able to hold my head up and build a life I loved that I was proud of. I didn't tell my parents what had happened to me until I was twenty-one, by that point I was grown and living on my own with a great job and a steady boyfriend.

When they asked me why I didn't say anything and why didn't I trust them to protect me my answer was simple— it would have ruined all our lives. They never would have looked at me the same, I would have been made to see counselors and therapists, and at the end of the day, this series of unfortunate events would have overtaken my life and all of theirs. I didn't want that. I knew somehow by the grace of God I was smart enough and strong enough to overcome it alone. And I did.

With God all things are possible, and I give HIM the glory for turning my private pain into a triumph.

When I did confess to my mother what Melissa did, she cried of course, but she told me something startling...

She had overheard once in our backyard the sounds of Melissa struggling in her house while the windows were open. She heard Melissa's stepfather forcing himself on her. Mom called out to ask if she was alright and everything went silent.

It's my family's opinion Melissa was being raped by her stepfather, with her mother's permission. Because of this she then did the same to me as a power play— so she could feel as though she had control over something in her life. I've been able to forgive Melissa through this discovery and much prayer. I hope she's well and happy wherever she is. She was a child too, and as the saying goes 'hurt people, hurt people.'

I just pray her hurting stopped as mine did.

My abuse story is just a snapshot of a small time period, but it's not my life story. It's not even remotely one of the top ten most interesting things about me. It was something that happened that I was able to overcome with much prayer and faith in God and I have become stronger by having experienced it.

- Leslie Alexander, 30's, Delaware, Oh

Abuse by definition is the mistreatment of people or animals in a mental, physical, sexual or emotional manner. For those of us though, who have experienced it firsthand, it means a great deal more.

I have personally experienced abuse as, unfortunately, I'm sure many of us have. Abuse is lying to family, friends, and coworkers about obvious injuries. Abuse is crying silently inside because it doesn't do any good to let the tears fall. Abuse is being convinced you're not enough, that you are a burden rather than a blessing. Abuse is failing in school or at work and people thinking your lazy when in reality, you're too busy trying to think of how to survive until the next day. Why didn't I get help? Why didn't I tell someone? Because as a child, I thought this was normal.... I thought this was normal. I thought I deserved it, that it was my fault.

Please know THIS IS NOT NORMAL, THIS IS NOT YOUR FAULT! Abuse happens when one person feels better about themselves when they have control of another.

My father was an abusive acholic, my mother was a workaholic who was never around. Years later, when the truth finally came out, no one could believe that this blue-collar American family was ever broken. My parents both had excellent jobs, we had a beautiful home in a nice neighborhood, and we always seemed happy. Until that spring day when the truth finally came crashing out...

It took many years of therapy to understand my abuse, to come to terms with the many horrible things that had happened to me and that I had no control. I'm now in my thirties, and while my father has not been in my life for a decade, the scars are still there, and it has affected me in many ways. I'm a very compassionate person, I feel because of the pain I have been through, I have a deeper empathy for any living creature. I'm also a victim of anxiety and depression, I have problems trusting and letting my walls down. I'm also single because of a perpetual fear of being owned by another human being.

Don't be afraid to get help, no one deserves to be abused in any way. You have no control over another human being's feelings, actions or intentions but you do have control of yourself. Save yourself, you are more valuable than you will ever know.

- K, Female, 20's Morgantown WV

I've come to believe love isn't a feeling or a cluster of emotion. Love is all about the action you partake in. Allowing yourself to fall in love with another person involves courage. Although that person doesn't know a love like yours, courage is choosing to fall in love anyway even if that means getting hurt and walking away less fortunate than you were when this whole love thing started out. To have courage is to be brave. When I think of the word courage, I think of jumping out of an airplane with a parachute but on an unexpected ride. You get on excited to reach your destination. Let your mind roam. A change in plans occur. Now your mind is racing, and all you can do is tell yourself you're gonna die from jumping or die staying aboard. You're thinking of all the terrible things that could happen when you feel a sudden nudge on your shoulder from the man behind you saying, "Hey kid, it's time" and you have no time to think until you're flying through the air never knowing what'll happen or where you'll land until it's over. When it is, all you can think is "damn."

Courage and faith walk hand in hand, especially within the story I'm about to share. At first, this was love. He was my first everything. It was a kiss you at stop lights, in the middle of the aisle, all the way through the movie kind of love. A show you off to my friends, hold every door including the car door open for you, sing you every word to every song I know with his hand on my knee the whole ride kind of love. We were together for about three years. Around our second anniversary, he began drinking. At first, he was just a cocky drunk. He couldn't be told anything, you couldn't talk to him, and he was uncompliant. But as the seasons changed and time went by, he would leave our little apartment, and I couldn't get a hold of him or find him anywhere as he had just started working for a seal coating and asphalt company where his coworkers and best friends were snorting cocaine and doing meth on the job site. I won't ever forget the look on his face with tear filled eyes the day he busted through my door all upset about the drugs his friends had fallen in love with. I begged him to quit but not even two weeks passed, and the man I loved was a man I'd never met.

The whites of his eyes were now a grayish yellow. His breath smelled like his mouth hadn't been open in weeks; stale. He refused to come to bed with me as he'd fall asleep on the couch drunk and wake up every morning in a puddle of urine. He hated me for just being alive. I began to pray. "God, if there is one thing in the world I need right now, it is you. Show me how to love this man enough to keep him alive and back to the Jake I fell in love with". Eventually, I got him to come to a Sunday morning service with me. That took courage and faith. I was so afraid he wouldn't bow his head for prayer, stand up for worship, and I figured he'd drop a cuss word at least once.

It actually went well, but he never returned. It was about that time things got physical. The first time it was for no reason. He was drunk and happy. We play fought and all the sudden he froze; no sign of life. He snapped out of it and hit me as hard as he could in my ribs more than once and rose his knife to my throat. "There is no way out." I don't remember being angry, telling my friends, or even leaving. I just remember feeling like an embarrassed, weak little girl.

The second time it was over our muddy dog and me not allowing her to ride with me to the dollar store. I was kicked in the back, thrown to the ground and locked out of my own house I, too, worked so hard for. Enough is enough. I blocked him on everything and left. He made over 20 different false numbers calling and texting me. One saying "I hope your family enjoys hide n seek. Your body will be placed in the trunk of every tree I pass." My friend read the message as I drove and I saw the horror in her eyes and the color drain her face. I begged for help, and the officer said he was a basic secretary with a badge and was unable to fix this. I lost it. What did I have to do? Die?

I continued to kill myself over a man who loved the high and drugs more than he could ever love me. I saw him at the bar with another girl after I had moved all my things back into our little home. I took a deep breath, and I ran inside screaming to the world of all the things he was doing to me. He spit in my face. My first reaction was to smack him. The bartender proceeded to call the police on me for assault. I realized when the cops swarmed the bar. I ran. I drove as fast as my little Buick could take me in hopes I could beat him home to pack my things with the help of a close friend. He beat me. "You've gotta go." The calmest voice I'd ever heard. I turned to face a stranger that I soon realized was the man I loved. I didn't recognize him. I sat unsettled. "We have to go." I lifted one foot to run toward the door but was picked up, slammed down, kicked in the chest and winded more than three times. I was blocked in. Courage. I decided to rise to my feet and win this fight or to die trying. I fought as hard as I could in hopes to knock him down so I could run. It never worked. I was tripped, and my head was stomped in with steel-toed boots on our pretty little porch. I don't know how I'm alive. All I know is God reached down and whispered "survive," and I did. I lived.

Courage was running for the car as he ran to the knives. Courage was going home to my mom's knowing he could find me quickly and easily there. Courage is writing this knowing he now lives right beside me and speaks of the death of me, still, ten months later. Courage is making yourself unmovable. Being rebuilt on a solid foundation after just barely piecing yourself back together. It is taking the extra step without seeing where the rest of the path leads but trusting your movements. Be unmoved. Be brave. Have faith and love yourself. Courage is something, often times, we don't see unless we are staring at it dead on in the rearview.

- Lindsey Adkins,
Newark, Ohio 20's

For two years, the physical and emotional abuse took a toll on me.

The very first incident was when he had totaled my car. He was fine, but the paramedics said I was lucky to walk away. I had a large piece of glass stuck in my neck and as we waited for the squad he grabbed the shirt a passerby had taken off their back to stop the bleeding and grasped the glass part tighter into my throat, demanding I take credit for the accident because at this point I was taking a huge risk on my life, while I suffered through the pain.

I was never okay with leaving due to being threatened constantly with my life.

From bruises to taking my breath away by strangulation, I never gave up hope. Even sheltered from my family. Many times, I wondered if it would have been easier to end it all, but I knew I had to gather the strength to face any consequences of going for help because my life had to have more meaning than that.

The thought was always there to go for help, every day of my life. Though the consequences always outweighed that until the final day.

I have had my hand broken, thrown into walls, given black eyes, burned with cigarettes and just been emotionally torn down for no reason other than drugs and anger issues. He needed his fix, and I was his enabler because I chose to not get beat on, so I continued giving him my paychecks. However, it never lasted. His friends would talk to me, and I'd simply reply with one-word answers but regretted it later. There was no stopping him.

Until the final end to the heartache:

He had kicked my windshield (shattering it) and grabbed me by my throat while I watched my face turn colors in the rearview mirror. Thank god, I realized my car was still in drive and managed to escape his grasp. There were handprints on my neck for quite some time, but the marks never overpowered the emotional side of things.

It's never easy being in these relationships. It takes time to heal. I suffer from PTSD, anxiety and panic disorders now, 8 years later.

Don't be afraid to run.

There are so many advantages to speaking up. It helps relieve built up betrayal, sadness, and anger. Though it isn't an overnight fix and the trauma haunts you forever, you'll find your inner peace and one day find the courage to forgive them, for your own sake.

Haven of Hope was a godsend for me. They were strong when I was weak.

There are places to go, people to protect you & things to benefit you.

Fast forward to the present...

I'm 26 years old with 3 beautiful girls, and though I still suffer from the emotional effects of that situation, my life has meaning. I have a purpose. My kids gave me hope for the future.

Find your purpose.

Your meaning.

Your new beginning.

- Dawn, 30's, Cambridge, Ohio

The Guidance counselor tells me a "Good union job down on the river" might be the best choice for me. I have also decided that vocational school and the drive back and forth are not the way to go either as the electronics course didn't cover anything except the installation of car stereos and basic multimeter use, so I approach the school to return to normal classes. They protest but agree to allow it to happen as long as they pick my course load and schedule. What I didn't know is, if they planned to not give me my diploma at the end at all and buried me in classes. Summer rolls around, and I'm shipped off to wrestling camp in Ann Arbor, Michigan. They were good to me there. Not mean at all. We worked hard but, it was actually a nice place to be.

12th grade. Alright, last run at this. Just as a side note, and to add insult to injury, in the midst of all this I'm figuring out that I'm attracted to guys and have a buddy I mess around with pretty regularly. So, that screws with my head even more. So, now I'm buried in classes. Spanish II, US History, World History, Geometry, Senior English, Government, Band, and Typing. Now throw in a job and wrestling. I'm barely staying afloat. My grades are shit. C's and D's mostly. I'm failing Spanish II and Geometry in the second grading period. I am now academically ineligible to be on the team. The coach has no choice but to kick me out. The result of this chain of events taught me the meaning of hatred. So, the news arrives at home. Dad is at school the next day in the principal's office. They agree to drop Spanish II from my schedule. I can graduate without it. Everything else stays. I remain ineligible for the next grading period, but that doesn't save me for the rest of the season. There are still two or three meets and the end of season tournaments after the next grading period.

Then I'm dragged in front of the coach with dad, and they agree to continue to allow me to practice with the team, although I cannot attend any meet in uniform. I just wanted to stay home and do my homework. NO. YOU WILL NOT BE A QUITTER. YOU WILL FINISH THIS. The next day, as per normal, the blood runs cold, practice begins. They used me for shark bait. (Shark bait means to have to wrestle everyone on the team for 1 minute, climbing 1 weight class each minute, until you drop from exhaustion or die). The assistant coach who was a former wrestler from a couple years before decided to get his two cents in at the end. Barely able to stand he beats me to the floor and grinds my face into the mat and asks me "why are you still here you faggot assed pussy retard" over and over.

I went home that night and threw all my gear at dad and cussed him like a sailor through the tears. Mom gets a little red and says she wants this son-of-a-bitches job. Dad goes to school the next day and gets in screaming match with the coach and the principal. It is agreed that this assistant will not speak or address me in any way and won't lay a hand on me. Practice continues. Grading period ends, and I'm now eligible due to the fact that I'm pounded for 2 hours a night with additional geometry homework that dad assigns himself. I have to wrestle off with the only other senior on the team for my place. I feel bad for the both of us. It was bloody and hateful. It was one of the few times I felt real motivation to win because the alternative was worse. In the end, I prevailed at 152 and Ben went to 160 even though we were the same size. I think I won 1 match and lost one before the Sectional tournaments.

Sectionals. I had planned to end it all there but ended up getting 3rd by mistake. My hair had gotten pretty long by this point, and I discovered that hair pulling even by accident could get you a point and win a match so, it was a weapon for my survival. That's what happened, and it turned the match and managed to place 3rd. So, shit. One more. One more week. Nobody's harassing me, beating me, threatening me, or otherwise giving me a hard time. District tournament arrives. I go and read the bracket. I luck out and catch my opponent in the hallway about 15 minutes beforehand. We've sparred a couple of times in the past, we're even. I tell him I'm tired and I want him to succeed. He wants this far more than I do. I only ask that he not intentionally injure me and the match is his. He agrees. The match proceeds as planned. He wins by 3 or 4 points, I can't even remember. I whispered thank you to him as we left the mat. I gained 15 pounds in less than 48 hours. Mostly water from dehydration.

From this point on and for the next 12 years, just to drive home the insanity and obsession, Dad would still try to harass me into conversations and speak of the matches as if they were only a week old. To this day he can name dates, times, events, and the names and teams of nearly all my opponents strictly from memory. This ended in 1996. Only in the last couple of years have I seen it finally start to recede and him cease to obsess. But my hatred for him remains. It has never faded.

- Male, 30's, Ohio

The worst part about abuse is that no matter where it starts, whether it be physically on the outside, sexually, or mentally from the inside, it manifests to each and every thought.

Every thought becomes about what you have been through. Why me? If I do one thing wrong will it happen again? Will everyone see me as less than normal now? You begin to feel like living in your own skin alone is cringe-worthy, like walking on eggshells.

Courage is to rise above your situation and emotions and look at reality. Courage is to realize your worth is not determined by anyone but you. Courage is realizing that no situation of your past or actions of another human being defines you. Courage is making your life what you want it to be because you know you are strong enough to overcome whatever comes your way.

My advice to a teen or anyone for that matter that is being abused is, don't be afraid to do what's necessary to get out of your toxic situation. There are still great people in this world. Share your story and don't feel guilty about taking time and learning to love yourself. There is a light at the end of the tunnel, and when you finally get there, you will know what it feels like to have a broken heart heal.

Being broken does not mean you are unworthy, it just means when all of your pieces come back together, finally, you are a masterpiece. There is a skill to learn in every situation brought upon us in life, and in abusive instances, your skill becomes a strength. Keep pushing forward.

- Brittaney S., 20's, Coshocton, Oh

I am going through so much right now: just starting a divorce, we have three kids, and he was with someone 12 days after we split up and has had our kids with her not letting me know until my daughter and a friend told me about it! Mad at me because I don't think it's right to have the kids around her yet (oh yeah, and he got drunk with her the night he had the kids. Both had accidents because they were camping and scared to go out to the bathroom because he was sleeping with his new girlfriend in his truck and had them in a camper. So, I had to clean them the next morning).

But we were together over 7 years, and he is now telling me he never loved me and calling me every name he can to hurt me! 7 years he has mentally beat me to the ground to the point I feel I'm not good enough for anyone! He has left me probably 10 times in that time frame but came back never said sorry just said we would work it out? He broke and trashed so many things in our houses. He checked himself into Chillicothe at the V.A. once, and he promised me that if I "okayed" his release, he would keep up with his counselor and medication. But he didn't, and it went bad again shortly after that! The kids and I were scared of him. We walked on eggshells, so to say, on a daily basis never knowing if he was going to flip out over something.

He didn't pay attention to the kids or me and if he did it normally wasn't good attention. He took over our bedroom and turned it into "his" room. The kids weren't allowed back there, he had his computer stuff in there, but that wasn't the reason, he just didn't want to deal with them!

I've slept on the couch for four years because he refused to take the locks off of the doors that went to our youngest daughter's room (she is only 4 now). But I didn't feel safe not being able to get to her quickly. We had already lost one house to a fire, so I am scared about things like that, but he still didn't worry that I slept on the couch while he was back in his room! And yes, he worked and paid the bills but that's what he wanted, he wanted me to stay home with the kids! But he ignored us if he had company over, his dad or friends, and they all went back to his room to "smoke." I don't do that, so I didn't fit in, so I just went about and did whatever. But if I ever had a friend over (I only have a couple), he was right out, normally staring at them like he was undressing them (that made me feel even shittier about myself). But then he would take over the conversation and talk to them, not me, and if I tried to talk, he always talked over me. So, I rarely had friends over!

But he could come and go as he pleased and be gone as long as he wanted with no explanation. He wouldn't watch the kids for me to go to the grocery store, so I had to take my girls with me. Caleb is 15, so he stays home. But if I went to my friend Dayna's house, it was always 20 questions: where? How long? What for? And, my goodness, if I stayed a little longer than expected he would be sooo pissed when I came home, he wouldn't talk to me!

And 7 years I was never allowed my own bank card, never put on any of his accounts, I was given an allowance, as he called it, for groceries and what was needed for the house! But he spent and bought what he wanted, when he wanted, and I never could question it.

He has mentally beat me down so bad, I should be happy we are apart, but it's really hard to hear him say he started sleeping with someone 12 days after we separated and that he never loved me! He is 32 his new girlfriend is like 18-20, I don't know, but it's his little sister's friend. She has a little girl, so he is now playing house with her! He is now threatening to shut off my cell phone, won't give me money to take the kids to lake/park this weekend, because his girlfriend will have her kid, so he wants ours to come play/babysit!

And he told me earlier he was done and not to ask him for anything anymore. He didn't care; it's not his problem anymore!! And I'm so sorry to bother you with this, but I just guess I want to know I'm not crazy and if anyone else thinks this shit is wrong? And also, I just need to vent to someone else who understands depression and what it truly feels like. My panic attacks have started again, but normally just sitting with my girls and having them rub my back and talk with them will ease them up! Again, sorry to bother you with all of my "drama" as he calls it.

- Lacey Boyer, 30's, Ohio

(Sent via messenger, and then I asked if she would like to have her story added to this book.)

ABUSE HELP INFORMATION

Sexual Assault
- National Sexual Assault Hotline: 800-656-4673
- Website: Rainn.org
- Website: Publichealth.org/resources/sexual-abuse
- Website: D2L.org/get-help/national-resources
- Phone: 866-367-5444

Domestic Violence
- Website: Domesticshelters.org
- Website: Womenshelth.gov
- Website: Loveisrespect.org
- Website: Bwss.org/resources/information-on-abuse/
- Website: Thehotline.org
- Website: Futureswithoutviolence.org

Child Abuse
- www.Childhelp.org
- 1-800-422-4453

BOOKS BY JACOB PAUL PATCHEN

Fiction

Sheltered: When a Boy Becomes a Legend
(upper middle-grade fiction, action/war, 2020)

Children's

Words That Matter
(children's picture book series, TouchPoint Press, 2019)

Poetry

Of Love and War
(poetry, Adelaide Books, 2018)

Creative Nonfiction

Life Lessons from Grandpa and His Chicken Coop
(creative nonfiction, family/inspiration, 2015)
Talking S. H. I. T. (Social, Humorous and Inspirational Thoughts)
(creative nonfiction, collaboration of social/humor blog, 2017)

See more of Jacob at Jacobpaulpatchen.com or on Facebook, Instagram, Twitter, LinkedIn, and YouTube.

NOTE FROM THE AUTHOR

Word-of-mouth is crucial for any author to succeed. If you enjoyed the book, please leave a review online—anywhere you are able. Even if it's just a sentence or two. It would make all the difference and would be very much appreciated.

Thanks!
Jacob

ABOUT THE AUTHOR

Jacob Graham, writing as Jacob Paul Patchen, is an Ohio writer who earns his inspiration through experience. He uses a unique voice of wit and grit to write about social issues, such as family, love, humor, learning, and war. Jacob is a five-star author of several books in various genres, an award-winning poet, and a combat veteran.

Thank you so much for reading one of our **Young Adult Fiction** novels.

If you enjoyed our book, please check out our recommended title for your next great read!

What the Valley Knows by Heather Christie

"A taut, compelling family tale." *-KIRKUS REVIEWS*

National Indie Excellence Awards- Young Adult Winner

Readers' Favorite Gold Medal Young Adult - Coming of Age

Maxy Awards Young Adult Winner

View other Black Rose Writing titles at www.blackrosewriting.com/books and use promo code **PRINT** to receive a **20% discount** when purchasing.